The L

MW01253511

and C ....

RICARA
FEATURES

Registered Kanienkeha:ka Kanonhsion:ni March 1994 (Julian Calendar)

Ricara Features, Grand River Territory, P.O. Box 269, Ohsweken, Ontario, Canada, NOA 1M0 *and* Ricara Features, via Tuscarora Nation, P.O. Box 664, Sanborn, New York, U.S.A., 14132-0664

All of these stories have appeared, some in slightly different form, exclusively in North American Indian periodicals and anthologies as follows: "Revelation," "Of Jewel's Choice," "The Red Moccasins," "Reunion," "The Smooth Water Pilgrimage," and "Flight," in *Turtle Quarterly*; "Of Jewel's Choice," (titled "Bronze My Skin, Dark My Eyes"), "The Smooth Water Pilgrimage," (titled "The Coming"), and "The Private Strangers," in *Indian Voice Magazine*; "Sometimes A Lonely Business," in *Indian Voice Magazine* and In Person: Variations, a contemporary literature program, (Harcourt Brace Jovanovich, New York); "The Last Raven," *Canadian Fiction Magazine*, All My Relations, An Anthology of Contemporary Canadian Native Fiction, (McClelland & Stewart Inc., Toronto), Native Literature, An Anthology of Canadian Native Literature in English (Oxford University Press, Toronto); "The Raspberry Chronicle," *Nativebeat* and *Turtle Quarterly*; "Resurrection," Returning The Gift Anthology, (University of Arizona); "A Jingle For Silvy," Studies in American Indian Literature, (California State University, Fullerton).

First printed in North America, June, 1994.
Hard cover ISBN 0-911737-03-0 Soft cover ISBN 0-911737-02-2

Dedicated to Mrs. Marion Green, my mother, who experienced the Mohawk Institute, a former government boarding school administered by the Anglican Church in Brantford, Ontario, Canada.

"We're afraid of what we don't know and
the Mohawks, largely because of our own
deliberate ignorance, are the unknown."
                              ---Michel Gratton,
                                   The Toronto Sunday Sun

Contents

Revelation

Fluttery snow flakes surprise the young couple; sunny, clear and warmer is the weekend forecast. Everything they own fits inside Mark's Honda Civic except two suitcases that are strapped to its roof. They work as a team, Mark is unloading, Sheryl is transporting. They are returning to the city from a delayed honeymoon trip.

Mark is undergoing a cultural renaissance. He wears a knitted sweater-coat with Mohawk symbols on it and encourages Sheryl to wear beaded things. He's convinced that the landlady likes Indians which is his explanation for the low price of their apartment rent. They are second generation academics fully able to exploit an advantage.

Sheryl totes their wedding gifts upstairs. These include matching moccasin slippers, two toasters, one coffee pot, one steam iron and six television lamps. She returns for a box of her Iroquois books and a small oil painting of a snarling wolf. Mark bought it from an art student friend after he learned that his mother belongs to the Wolf Clan. In the Rotinonhshion:ni system you are what your mother is.

Mark recently became aware that because they were married in a church, they aren't married according to the laws of their people.

He also found that if Sheryl is wolf clan, she isn't his wife, she is his sister. In future, even if they seek penance, she can *never* be his wife. That thought bothers him.

He pulls the suitcases from the roof and carries them toward the house. "Be careful of the painting," he says.

"He's too mean looking," Sheryl says, balancing it atop the box of her books. "That's what's wrong with it---too much of a stereotype."

A plump woman with greying hair stands on the front porch with arms crossed and Mark expects to be issued a house list of no-no's. Instead, after Sheryl goes inside, the landlady whispers: "You have pretty wife, Ja? How they say it. . .tall dark and handsome?"

Mark nods and realizes he must be blushing. Her remark has supplied pride that only a maiden husband can value.

"She has much beauty. . .and such a short skirt for dis cold vedder. I hope you vill be happy here."

Mark tucks a suitcase under an arm, gropes into his pants pocket and holds out a $50 bill. "Here's the money I owe you," he says. "I wanted to be sure I had enough for the trip. Better to be safe than sorry."

"Ja," she says. "But if you still have not enough money now, you can make up difference next month, Ja? Maybe that would be better arrangement. I'm sure beautiful Indianer wife has much to buy just getting started, no?"

"Are you sure it's okay?" He lowers his hand. "This won't cause *you* any hardship?"

"Nah."

"Well, I assure you that you'll get it with next month's rent."

"What is this ashure? What means this?"

"Assure means that you can be certain I'll give you the money."

"Oh," she smiles, clasping her hands. "I trust you. I ashure you will."

They carry their stuff upstairs to the second floor and go inside apartment number three. When Mark kicks the chocolate coloured door closed, Sheryl bounds ahead of him. He has to turn sideways to climb the sharply inclined stairway. He stumbles and catches himself between step five and six. Above a small landing, the kitchen comes complete with railing, table, hot-plate, sink and small refrigerator. This is the only room in the small, attic apartment where Mark can stand up.

He bends down and goes into the bedroom. Sheryl is lying on the floor atop a tattered mattress and is peering through a small window. She's looking beyond three rooftops at a golf course. Mark puts the suitcases next to a painted bureau, takes off his coat and dives for the mattress.

"Mark? Am I seeing things or are there golfers down there in the snow?"

Mark snuggles next to her and props his head up. "That must be the Polar Bear Tournament I read about in the paper this morning. I guess that's where the Municipal Golf Course is."

"Have you ever played golf?" Sheryl turns to him.

"I don't think I'm going to tell you," he gently bites her nose. "You see, what's fair is fair. You have your little secret and now I have mine."

Sheryl pulls away like a miffed cat and continues to spectate. Mark wonders if she knows what clan she is.

"You can only be ano:wara, okwaho or okwari you know: turtle, wolf or bear."

"Since when do you know the language?"

"I don't. I just know the clans. What's yours?"

Sheryl huffs on the window and it fogs. She continues the huffing until she's frosted the whole window. "There's your answer---get it?"

"Okay." Mark wipes the window with a forearm. "I learned to play golf when I worked as a caddy. Someday, when you've been

a good little girl and told me your clan, I might even teach you
how to hit a golf ball."

"I played softball on the Rez, remember? I already know how to
hit."

"You know how to swat, not hit. There's a big difference. It's
called finesse."

Sheryl squeaks the glass with her fingers. "Suddenly, you seem
to be Mr. Expert on everything. . ."

"You can slice it, top it, sky it, hook it, shank it or miss it. But
every once in a while you connect with it just right and it goes, oh,
how it goes." He rolls sideways and kisses her temple. "That's
what makes everything in life worthwhile," he slaps her buttocks,
"when you make that perfect connection."

"Owww," Sheryl says. "Do you always act like a madman?"

He grabs a pillow and begins swatting her head. "Yes," he says.
"And it's all because of you. You drive me mad, Mad, MAD, do
you hear me?"

Wrestling with Sheryl became Mark's favourite pastime during
their junior year at University. Sheryl's tall and though frail she's
surprisingly strong when excited or angry. Once, she almost
broke Mark's arm during one of their matches. As they roll off the
mattress her sweater pulls up.

"Belly button!" Mark begins tickling her navel.

Sheryl reaches for the pillow. As her long, black hair sweeps
across his face, he feels a sharp thump. Pain shoots through his jaw
and his eyes begin watering. He pushes her away, sits up on his
knees and wipes his eyes.

Sheryl rubs the heel of her hand. "Damn you," she says. "You've
hurt my hand."

"*I*'ve hurt *your* hand?"

"Yes you," she says yanking her sweater down.

She gets Marks attention by twiddling her fingers as if warming
up to play concert piano, clenches them into a fist and punches

Mark's nose. She leaps to her feet and bolts for the door. Mark lunges and snags an ankle. He pounces upon her, securing her wrists so she can't use her claw-like fingernails. He feels her body stop struggling; hardness and tightness loosen. Thoughts of war become irrelevant; he's taken by an opposite thing and releases her wrists.

"Do you like it here?" He helps Sheryl up and bumps his head.

She puts a suitcase on its side, unbuckles the snaps and pulls open a bureau drawer. "You can have the two top drawers," she says. "You're taller."

He decides to let the question pass. He feels guilty about the dingy apartment but whose fault is that? They were supposed to marry one *year* after he graduated, not one month. He watches her fitting clothes into the drawer. He thinks: my beautiful wife condemned by me to a prison sentence in this horrid apartment.

He clears his throat. "Maybe you could brighten the place up somehow," he says. "We could really use a radio."

She begins putting sweat pants into the drawer. "It doesn't have a wood stove."

He moves behind her. "What?"

"I like this apartment, even if it doesn't have a wood stove."

"Do you really?" He hugs her. "You're not putting me on?"

"It's sort of like, well, like a penthouse."

"I wouldn't exactly call it a penthouse."

"Maybe not, but it's the first thing we're sharing. I mean, don't you think that's important?"

Mark nods, burrows his face into her hair and kisses the nape of her neck. A box of wedding presents is on the floor. He says: "I guess we'll have to buy a television. . .no, six television sets. That way we'll have one for every TV lamp."

"Why not just have one TV with six lamps on top of it?"

"Impossible my dear," Mark says in his best English accent. "We'd need too many recepts."

"Huh?"

"Receptacle, you know, the female electrical wall outlets where you put the plug in. . .the male and the female. . .in and out. . ."

". . .Oh. . ."

"Anyway, your suggestion minimizes each's importance by one-sixth."

"Yes, but we extend their life six times."

"Poppycock." He reaches into the suitcase and hands her three shirts. "That's purely an assumption on your part. You can't say you've extended their lives equally because each is different."

"They're not the same design, but all have the same wattage in their bulbs. Kind of like people, don't you think?"

"Well if I were a TV lamp, I'd want my own television set. That's what I was created for and that's what I'd want."

She stuffs the shirts into the drawer. "You mean you wouldn't want to share it?"

"No."

"Oh-wow! Are you kidding? You'd actually be selfish enough to hog your own. . ."

"Selfish? That's not being selfish. That's uh, well fulfilment of purpose. Like a pregnant woman."

Sheryl's brown eyes widen. "You've been in the city too long---you've turned into an apple."

Mark doesn't want to believe she's serious despite her forbidding look. He considers these little skirmishes an entertainment and can't see her as an adversary to anything. "You realize that we'll have one lamp left over, eh Sheryl?"

"What?"

"After we place each lamp, with its very own TV in every room including the bathroom, we'll have one left over. Where do you want to put it? Which room will get two?"

Her brow pushes into a frown. "None." In a low, deliberate tone she says, "The stairway is an equal to the others. It should go there no-matter-what."

"I'm glad you see it my way," Mark frowns to mimic her.

"Who's going to make the choice? Who's going to play the Creator?"

"What do you mean?"

"Who's going to make the decision as to which lamp goes where?"

"Well," Mark clears his throat. "I suppose the choice will be determined by the decor of the room. It really doesn't matter. . ."

"Since you're King of this castle, I guess you'll want to put the luxurious marble Venus in the living room. That'll be the most appropriate spot for her---don't you think?"

Mark's never considered himself King of the castle but he's taken by the ring of title. He decides to let it stand so he can find out where Sheryl's going with this. He bows majestically.

"The glass glove can go in the far room. I guess you'll want Cupid in the bedroom. That leaves the Chinese Buddha, the black stableboy and the covered wagon. Where do you want those placed, Your Highness?"

"I think the covered wagon should go in the stairway landing." Mark smiles. "Stairs suggest travel, don't you think?"

She nods and pushes aside a wisp of hair. "Continue," she says. "You're doing just fine."

"I, uh, I guess the Buddha can go in the kitchen. After all, we know the Chinese are cooks which is exactly what you'll be doing in the kitchen." Mark studies Sheryl for a clue of some sort; he's not sure where she's taking him.

She says: "That leaves the black stableboy to live in the bathroom?"

"Yes," Mark nods. "In a way, bathrooms are nothing more than human stables anyway."

"I see," Sheryl says. "A place for everything and everything in its place. That's what kind of marriage I can expect?"

"I wouldn't say that. . ."

The bottom door opens and the shuffling and slapping of floppy shoes echoes up from the stairwell. "Yoo-hoo! I'm coming to told you about the wash back!"

"It's the landlady," Mark whispers. "Come on."

He takes Sheryl's hand and tugs her toward the kitchen. They peer through the doorway as the landlady is scuffling across the floor. A plunger rests on her shoulder as if it were a rifle.

"I'm sorry," the landlady says, her face is creased with concern. "I'm sorry I'm interrupting nice, young, Indianer couple but I'm coming to check bathroom for wash back."

In unison they say: "What's wash back?"

They follow her to the lavender bathroom. Sheryl studies its cramped interior. Two-inch vertical boards divide cracked plaster walls and rusty pipes poke up through the floor. The landlady jabs the plunger into the toilet bowl and sings something in a foreign tongue which is barely audible above the sucking and sloshing. Grey water quickly becomes infested with floating curds.

"I'm having to check dis john," the landlady proclaims. "Las' time snow is melting, dis toilet had wash back and flooded on the floor. Plumber-man is saying he'll be here Munday to fix-em up. He says plunging is fixing it okay until he comes, long as dis new snow doesn't melt." She's plunging so hard the whole bowl is rocking. Mark imagines the connection snapping and all of them washing downstairs in the tide.

"There," she says. She pushes the handle and the toilet gurgles into action. "If he's plugging up just use dis plunger. I'll leave it here until it's fixed, Ja?" She walks across the kitchen and ka-thumps downstairs. "Sorry I'm bothering you." She slams the door.

"P-U." Sheryl turns away. "Now I know why we had outside toilets on the Rez. We definitely need an air freshener around here."

Mark bends down to follow Sheryl back into the bedroom.

Mimicking the landlady, he says: "I'm wondering if nice ole land-lady is coming upstairs every time spirit is moving her, Ja?"

"Oh-wow," Sheryl says. "She's priceless isn't she? She must be Hungarian or Romanian with that thick accent, eh?"

"It's obvious to me that she's German."

Sheryl takes two blouses from the suitcase, puts them into the drawer and closes it. "I think she's a beautiful old lady. Really beautiful."

"Maybe she's a Russian with a fake German accent to throw everybody off. Wouldn't it be funny if she's a KGB agent and this house is under CSIS surveillance?"

"Get serious. It doesn't matter what her origin is as long as she's of a good mind."

"She's good minded all right," Mark says. "She's letting us owe her fifty dollars until next month---and it was her idea."

Sheryl flops the suitcase closed and slides it into the closet. As she bends over, Mark watches panty lace outline the crescents of her buttocks to form an inverted heart. She seldom wears panty-hose, the smoothness of her legs and their colouring don't require them.

"Speaking of origin," he says. "I'll bet you three TV lamps that you don't know what clan your mother is."

Sheryl settles on the edge of the mattress and jerks her skirt down. "That's so important to you isn't it?" Her eyes shrink into slits.

"Well, uh, no." Mark shrugs and sits down beside her. "But I think I should know."

"Why is it so important that you know?"

"Well uh. . ." Mark considers telling her the real reason and its consequences. Instead, he says: "What if my relatives or the In-dians down at the Friendship Centre should ask. . ."

"Get real; they won't care."

". . .am I supposed to say I don't know?"

"Why not tell them I'm a Pisces, you know, the white man's fish clan? No, better yet---tell them that I'm a bear. That's my clan. Just tell them that I'm truly a bear, a growling bear to go with your snarling wolf."

"Sheryl---you're being very childish"

"No I'm not. You can keep me in the bathroom with the stable-boy. That way you'll only have to see me out of necessity. But most of the time, except when you need me for cooking or bed, I'll be conveniently out of sight."

Mark creeps over to the window. While the echo of her words slowly diminish, he watches heavy snowflakes, mixed with rain, quickly falling. They cover the rooftops and the golf course and begin turning accumulated snow into slush.

Some of the golfers turn up their collars or pull ear flaps down from their caps. Others take out gloves and rain hats from golf bag compartments. Some replace their black golf balls with daylight fluorescent ones. After making these adjustments, they continue their play oblivious to conditions.

Mark twists his body to gaze at his bona fide wife. A discernible smile of joy marks his relief.

The Raspberry Chronicle

This is an almost true story about history and Indians. It's also about a seer named Ronald Maple. In addition, I guess you could say it's about freedom and the lessons that can be learned from it. Native people watch for the medicine in life very carefully. It teaches us things.

Did I really know a seer? I surely did. Of course when I first met him, he wasn't into his seer mode yet. He was born Ronald Joshua Maple and raised on the Akwesasne Reserve. Like many of his Mohawk relatives before him, he had learned to climb the steel for good wages and eventually settled in San Francisco. That's where I met him and his dainty Costanoan wife.

Costanoan Indians lived on the south shore of what became San Francisco Bay. Though their shamanism has passed away with scarcely a trace, we know that their doctors could sing, dance and suck material objects out of the body of the sick. Sometimes they exercised control of the weather and of the natural crops. Looking back on things now, that connection was vital to what happened. And to what didn't happen.

Ronald never graduated from high school yet he talked like one of those graduate students from across the Bay in Berkeley. In the late sixties, Students for a Democratic Society at the University of California began exercising so much freedom, straight people started referring to the place as Berserkly. Nary a day went by when the flower child movement, whose capital was the corner of Haight and Ashbury Streets in San Francisco, drew a generation of young people from around the globe. These new freedom fighters fondled beads and each other and wore Indian headbands.

Real North American Indians were suddenly deemed heroes and became revered saviours. So when Native people recaptured Alcatraz Island, an abandoned federal prison in San Francisco Bay, a whole generation of peace began spreading throughout North America. Just like in Iroquoian and other Native prophesies. And in the prophesies, a young leader comes forth to guide the people out of despair and back to the spiritual path the Creator gave them.

Though all this was clear to me, Ronald couldn't be convinced to participate in history. He'd push his black, wavy hair from his eyes and his round face would become rounder as he smiled at the thought. It didn't matter to him that abandoned government property is legally supposed to revert back to the indigenous people of the area.

I knew fear of being arrested couldn't be the reason for his refusal to come down to Pier 38 and board the launch for Alcatraz with the rest of us. Though of a placid nature, his stocky body hinted at lacrosse prowess and he'd been in scrapes with the law before. Once at an Indian rights demonstration, I saw him walk right up to a frightened cop, shake hands with him and put his arm around the startled officer. Then he laughed it off and everybody became friendly. With the whole Bay Area rushing to support their new heroes would the government dare remove a few upstart Indians and make us into martyrs? Of course not. None of these arguments swayed Ronald from his no-action decision.

You'd have thought that with all those learned college students taking part, somebody would have figured out an occupation strategy. Not that they were high or anything; drugs and alcohol were strictly forbidden. Consensus determined that if The People were spiritually of one mind, rightness would happen without manipulation. Luckily, somebody did figure out that we needed spiritual guidance to pull this operation off so medicine people were beckoned. I went to pick them up at San Francisco International Airport.

They came from Ontario, Quebec, New York, Oklahoma, Arizona and South Dakota. Craggy, austere, elderly old men who know the secrets of the universe and how to guide their people through spiritual land mines. They came to Alcatraz straight from the harvests of October with their pouches brimming with fresh, potent medicines from all of the four directions. And they burned tobacco with the Hippies and the young people from the Indian nations and they smoked.

Some say that's not the reason they came at all. And I suppose if you choose to see it, you would say they really came for another purpose. They really came to save Ronald from going to the spirit world. Temporarily at least.

Now I won't say us Mohawks are stubborn, determined seems a better word, but once we get something in our craw, or go to war, it's not over until we get satisfaction. You literally have to hit us over the head to make your point and that's exactly what happened to Ronald.

By this time he had come over to the island out of curiosity and to visit with newly arriving friends. People were always glad to see him; his presence uplifted them. He always had a good word and smile for everybody. White people of the Bay area shipped food, supplies and money to the island. In a kind of reverse Thanksgiving celebration, Pilgrims took turkeys and all the trimmings to the Indians. For a few short months, peace may not have made it throughout the rest of the world but it sure had a foothold on Alcatraz Island. Then Ronald sort of got killed.

Some kind of drug deal went down in a mainland pool hall in
The City. Nobody knew why Ronald happened to be there, but he
got swatted on the head with the handle of somebody's pool stick.
They rushed him to the hospital but he lay in a coma and somehow
it became my duty to take the medicine men to him for doctoring.

We sat in the hallway for two days trying to gain entry to
Ronald's room. Finally, after being legally declared dead, I guess
they figured they had nothing to lose. They let us inside and a
doctor and nurse watched the medicine ceremony that took place
through the windows in the double-doors. When the tag on Ronald's big toe started to wiggle, the nurse collapsed from her
window. She had passed out and after Ronald came to, I heard the
doctor ask one of the elders how they did it. He offered them
$50,000 to teach him "this trick" but everybody politely smiled
and helped Ronald to his feet. Surprisingly, we didn't have to
sign any release papers or official documents or anything. Our
whole group just quietly left the quietest hospital I've ever been in.

Aside from a noticeable limp, Ronald seemed sort of troubled
in his new life. Oh, he didn't appear that way at first. He just kind
of went north to rest at his wife's house on her reservation. But
when he came back to Alcatraz, he was like an anxious soldier at
his battle station waiting for action.

A lot of people pledged help during the occupation but few
focused on the Indian cause. Ronald and a committee listened to
proposals that were supposed to make everybody rich but when
businessmen found out that greed wasn't the motive for the occupation, some became indifferent. None proved worthy of the lofty
educational goals and objectives set by The People so they were
politely escorted to the boat dock and shuttled back to the mainland.

One day, Ronald's face bore the look of a man at peace as he
hobbled up the incline back to his prison cell. When I asked him

to tell me what he had in his mind he said that it hadn't come to him yet. He told me to stay tuned and when it did, I'd be the first to know. If he considered applying for grants to develop Alcatraz he'd need some volunteers to help.

Prison cells at Alcatraz hold the cold very well. Dampness from the fog gets you; it gets into your bones and sitting close to a fire is the only remedy. So we had a People's Fire every night and drummed and exchanged tribal songs and became bonded brothers and sisters. After the medicine men went home, a lot of Indians left the Island and never came back; it seemed like there were more Hippy people than Indians. Could their belief in freedom through pleasure top our belief of freedom to survive?

Discussions turned to arguments and just when all seemed lost Ronald told me he had a dream to tell. It didn't matter that there weren't any medicine people around to hear it. Ronald said he could translate the dream himself.

This had all happened before. Sir Frances Drake's men had brutalized the gentle, Costanoans in 1579. He said they took a boat load of Indians to Alcatraz for execution but that his kindred spirit had saved them. After using the fog for cover, he threw two guards to the sharks and while helping a woman and her child to safety, something sucked him down into the water. He went darker and darker into the deeps until a glowing, blue light seemed to enlighten his mind. He could see aquaculture and ways to harvest seaweed. He saw how the fertile ocean floor could be turned into commercial raspberry orchards. After viewing these inspiring secrets, buoyancy forced him to the surface.

I wondered why he told me these things. Before I could ask, he hobbled off the island and went to the reservation and I didn't see him again for two months. When I went to visit, he took me into an old shed. I saw scale models of bubble-like greenhouses and my mouth must have been open in amazement because he laughingly told me they were underwater raspberry greenhouses; the first of their kind. He said that the controlled atmosphere chambers literally put the fruit asleep. When modified atmosphere packaging is used, the notorious short shelf life of the raspberry is overcome. Anybody listening would have thought Ronald had a master's degree in horticulture. I knew different.

He said that research at the University of Manitoba proved that raspberry juice could be extracted using a filtration process that required no heat treatment. The juice and puree option and longer shelf life made extensive raspberry farming a possibility. Since a raspberry grower has a potential gross of $4,000 per acre, Indian growers could expect a greater profit margin due to excused taxes.

"We're all going to become raspberry experts and survive according to the Creator's wishes," Ronald said with a smile. "You know, our people used to do Raspberry Dance but we quit. Now it's time to reinstate it.

"We'll convert these buildings into a major raspberry processing plant and divide the profits equally. Nobody's job is more important; everybody's equal under our Creator's Great Law."

I really thought he could pull it off. He went to all the local Indian communities to organize people for raspberry production. He reminded them that their small Reservations and Rancherias made raspberries the perfect cash crop for them. He intended to start in California and go east so every tribe could accept his survival concept. No longer would the people be subservient to the whims of others. A new west wind was blowing, heralding the return of the Buffalo, just like in the ancient prophesies.

I wrote a short proposal for him and delivered it to a well-connected San Francisco lawyer. Over dinner he told me Ronald had a problem.

Ronald's two young cousins had arrived from Akwesasne to visit. They lived at the reservation and began hanging out at a private summer camp about six miles away. Some of the people knew all about the marijuana growers who rented land on the reservation for a pittance and pocketed large profits. Some of the young men would wait until harvesting and then go and steal whatever they needed for a fast buck. This led to armed camps and mean dogs which were used to protect a grower's stash. But Ronald's cousins weren't attracted to marijuana plants. They were attracted to horses.

Since the summer camp had stables which were in a remote wooded area, they began sneaking horses out for free rides. When the manager of the camp found out about it he took his gun to the boys. After opening fire and containing them for an entire afternoon, they finally escaped and told Ronald. After a confrontation and argument, the manager threatened to kill Ronald and his cousins if they ever set foot at the summer camp again. The lawyer deduced that the camp was really a front for a marijuana farm.

One night at eight o'clock my telephone rang. The same medicine men that had been on Alcatraz Island were coming back to California. This time they were coming to conduct a Longhouse funeral for Ronald Maple. Would I pick them up at the airport? I swallowed hard, cleared my throat and uttered a faint, "yes."

Standing in the road in the rain, the medicine men conducted a tobacco burning ceremony. That's pretty strong stuff because it's a direct line Rotinonhshon:ni have to the Creator. A chalked outline of Ronald's body was marked on the road but one of the medicine men knew different. Ronald was actually killed on the entrance road to the stables and dragged thirty feet off camp property up to the county road. The traditional chief of the reservation saw the camp's manager wielding a gun and standing with Ronald and a cousin on camp property when he drove by. After Ronald sent his cousin home, shots were fired. His cousin crept back and found Ronald's body laying face down on the road.

A traditional funeral was held at the reservation in the shed. Tipped on its side, the raspberry greenhouse scale model rested

against the wall. Ronald's spirit was fed and set free to leave in
peace for the spirit world. Then his body went back to Mother
Earth under the redwood trees at the burial grounds. Because it's
so shady and damp in the redwood forest, plastic flowers are put
on people's graves. Plastic flowers were placed on Ronald's
grave.

According to testimony, Ronald lunged at the camp manager
from behind a tree with a knife. A self defense verdict set the
manager free. With Ronald's handicap, such a mighty leap from
behind any tree near the site would have been impossible. Even
for an Olympic athlete. The prosecuting attorney never called the
traditional chief as a witness. Reporters didn't want to go up into
the rugged boondocks of the reservation so as usual, few Indian
voices were heard.

For almost two years the Alcatraz occupation continued then
things went dim and everybody went home; some being forcefully
removed. As for the prophesy, a new west wind of change is blowing over the world. Aquaculture and raspberry growing is an idea
that is just starting to catch on. But not in Indian Country.

As for the Hippy freedom children? They too seemed to evapo-
rate but some found pleasures of a different sort. Recently, Cyril
Hoffman, one of the revolutionary leaders of Students for a Democratic Society back at Berkeley in the seventies got arrested for
speeding. In his Rolls Royce.

Of Jewel's Choice

Jewel's name fit snug as a moccasin. Her skin shone with the richness of cured tobacco; eyes sparkled like fine crystal. From the very first, her family called her Precious but while in elementary school, she decided not to respond to anything incorrect. It didn't take long for everybody to get her message.

Her parents, who were progressives, sought to give her every advantage and after she completed the Reserve school, mother drove her fifteen miles every day to high school in the city. The modern world couldn't be denied and they wanted her prepared to cope with it.

Jewel completed her studies with honours and attended a large university. She learned Christianity, was encouraged to frequent as many social functions as possible and successfully eluded many who wooed her. Yet even when she graduated she remained troubled, unfulfilled. She didn't want to hurt her parent's feelings, especially her mother's, so she never revealed the doubts that festered inside.

At family gatherings, mother would boast, "Jewel is the first one of us to receive the white man's degree." And all the relatives politely nodded their approval allowing her mother to swell with pride. Only grandfather, a condoled Chief with a Mohawk title read the truth in her eyes.

Jewel couldn't pinpoint her dilemma. When she went into the woods with her friends to gather medicinal herbs, she felt silly. After all, *she* was educated and not once during all those years of schooling had any instructor ever taken her into the woods to look for roots and leaves. Besides, she wasn't very good at it. All the other girls knew where to probe but Jewel seemed only capable of finding strawberries and hickory nuts.

At twenty-two she took a summer job pumping gas at a Reserve convenience store owned by a cousin. Though she soon became bored with her mundane tasks, she met a young lacrosse player named Titus Joshua. He was not turtle clan which, according to the old way, made him an eligible suitor.

Tie, as he preferred to be called, bristled with masculinity; his body beamed vitality during their frequent moonlight swims down at the river. Everybody said: "They make such a handsome couple." And sooner than most expected, Jewel was with child and wedding plans were hastily arranged.

Tie's uncle, a wolf clan faith keeper in the Longhouse, assumed his chief would perform a wedding ceremony in the traditional way but Jewel's parents said no. They had become devout, born-again Christians and refused to allow their daughter to be married in the old way. In order to save the situation, Jewel was forced to practise one of the things she learned in school.

"But Tie," she purred one moonlit evening down at the river. "It's not that I don't respect your uncle or even the old ways. It's just that, well, what about the baby? White people consider a fatherless child illegitimate you know."

"Ha, ha, ha. Don't be silly," Tie said. "How can any child be fatherless?"

"If we don't have a church wedding we won't be legally married. And if we're not legally. . ."

"For a smart girl, you sure are dumb. This is the Reserve. If they don't recognize our laws that's their problem, eh?"

"Now Tie, think of the baby; think of your son. If we're not legally married he won't be entitled to your name or his inheritance.

"Inheritance?"

"When you become a great lacrosse player and make a lot of money, things like inheritance will become very important to him. You don't want everything taken away from your own flesh and blood do you?"

Tie was pensive. Though not materialistically inclined Jewel had watched his eyes reflect what she interpreted as visions of fame and fortune.

"Nobody's going to take anything away from my kid," he said. "But I just can't do it. It would be too much of a disappointment to my Uncle."

"Then we'll have two ceremonies." Jewel took his hand. "One by your uncle's chief and another in my mother's church. That should make everybody happy," she nibbled on his ear.

But when they stood before Tie's uncle and told him of their plan he said: "If you are married in the Indian way there's no reason for any additional ceremonies. Putting signature to a piece of paper doesn't make love the truth. Truth can only come from a pure heart."

Tie looked at his uncle. "She's four months pregnant."

Jewel blurted, "But we love each other; we're getting married out of love---not necessity."

Tie's uncle turned to Jewel. "I want to tell you something you should know," he said quietly. "Our Grandmother Moon has much spiritual power. She and she alone controls the tides of the great salt waters. It is her job to remind Mother Earth to observe the four seasons and to prepare for them. She also counsels the feathered and four-legged ones in their duties, exerting her influence so they remain on their intended paths.

"Just as she does all these things, once a month she reminds women they are blessed with the power to bear children. Because of this, women are closer to Grandmother Moon than men. But she also recognizes that during this time a woman's spiritual power may be disturbed. Now that you are with child, portions of your power are being diverted to the little one in your belly. The melting of two people into one in marriage demands all of the power within you. There should be no discrepancies; better wait until the baby's born."

Jewel felt hurt. In her whole life she couldn't remember any occasion when she experienced rejection. "Then I guess we'll get married in the Christian way," she said.

Tie's uncle remained serene. "When I need guidance," he said softly, "I go into the woods and pray to the Creator. Then, I pay attention to any messages He might send me."

"What kind of messages does He send?"

"I don't know---that's between you and him," he smiled. "Maybe nothing, ha, ha, ha."

Jewel decided to go into the woods to appease Tie and to show respect for his uncle. To complete the mockery, she determined to abandon her city clothes for this journey and she pouted. She had grown fond of lacy, feminine things; knew they enhanced her beauty. Those old animal skins made her look plain and besides, they were awfully heavy. With reluctance, she changed into a buckskin dress and put on her moccasins. Over her shoulders, she draped a white shawl trimmed with lace. To grandfather's questioning eyes she explained: "I need it to keep warm." She departed into the bush behind her house.

She didn't expect to be gone very long so instead of gathering firewood, she used the shawl to carry berries she picked along the way. When darkness sifted among the tree trunks, she realized her error; fire should have been first priority. She hadn't camped outside for ten years and huddled against the trunk of a pine. Sparkles of star light broke through the rustling branches above and her pulse quickened.

Suddenly, the wind gusted and the forest came alive with moaning, bending sounds. Pine cones pelted the ground and one grazed her cheek. It seemed like she had been scratched by a giant, invisible finger. Branches flapped like great eagle wings, sending a flurry of pine needles to pepper her head. A twig snapped and two luminous eyes appeared. Grandfather always said that the animal race and Onkwehon:we were friends but was she still Onkwehon:we?

When the wind stopped, the eyes disappeared as if by signal. Jewel wished she hadn't come; she felt stupid. She curled into a ball, wrapped herself in the shawl, and promised herself she'd leave at first light.

At dawn, she realized her task wouldn't be easy. Because of her attention to berry picking, she couldn't recognize a single landmark. She considered her predicament and decided not to panic; she'd use her education to figure things out. She recalled reading that moss always grew on the north side of tree trunks. She gingerly threaded her way though the woods checking for moss.

Jewel felt the irritation in her parched throat as the sun reached high noon. She stopped to massage her aching feet and saw a pine tree that looked familiar. Upon inspection, she realized she had come full circle---she was back where she started. Tears streamed down her cheeks while she scooped pine needles into a mattress. She fluffed the shawl into a pillow and fell asleep.

In late afternoon, wistful thoughts of Tie danced in her memory. She could feel something watching; it must be him; he'd come on his white horse to rescue her. She jumped to her feet and rubbed her eyes in disbelief. A herd of deer surrounded her; their big ears twitching to ward off flies. Though their dots were almost gone, fawns stayed near their mothers and a stag stood, his horns still temporarily coated with velvet. He stared at Jewel, thrust out his chest and strutted off.

A doe came forward with glassy, questioning eyes. Jewel froze. She saw a tree branch low enough to climb but three deer blocked her way. As the doe moved closer, its big eyes became hypnotic. Jewel began trembling. Her belly growled and the doe pricked up its ears. Though her heart pounded, she felt cold.

She picked up the shawl and draped it around her shoulders. To her surprise, the doe abruptly turned and began walking away. One by one, as if sensing some sort of danger, the deer disappeared into the woods.

Jewel breathed a sigh of relief, found a sharp stone and nicked tree trunks to mark her trail. She felt foolish at being lost so close to home. As the sun sank beneath the horizon, she found a familiar road and hurried along its dusty shoulder. Sharp stones pierced her moccasins and she plucked burdocks from hair and shawl. Her feet bled but she couldn't feel any pain. Tie would marry her in a church and they would move to the city. She limped down her lane, hobbled into the house and went straight to her room. Though her parents were glad to see her, she was too embarrassed to give them any details of her journey. She regretted having done such a foolish thing.

Yet when Tie brought his uncle to her home later that evening, Jewel fluffed a pillow against the headboard of her bed and said: "I'm so glad to see you." She spoke in a whisper. "As you probably know, my parents are upset with me for going through with your suggestion. They were afraid I'd lose the baby and harsh words were exchanged." She clasped Tie's hand and pulled him to her side. "I thought you'd come for me in the woods. . ."

"No," Tie's uncle said. "You're the only one that can do it." He sat at the foot of her bed. "Tell me what happened to you."

Jewel began her story and emphasized every detail of her journey. She expected their sympathy and wanted them to fully understand the agony she had suffered. She believed nothing could be read into it, after all, she hadn't experienced any uplift of heart. When she finished, she drew her hand away from Tie's and folded her arms across her bosom.

Tie's uncle stood up. "I think something happened to you," he said. "Consider that on the first night you weren't yet humble enough to receive His message, so the wind accomplished that purpose. When the eyes saw that you had become receptive, you were allowed to sleep.

"On the second day, when you grew impatient and tried to leave prematurely, you were returned to where you started. Deer were sent to communicate to you and when you scared them off, you completed their message."

"Scared them off?" Jewel sat forward. "I, / scared them off?"

"When you covered yourself with the machine-made cloth shawl they became confused at your identity and retreated.

"Do you really think. . ."

"Our brothers of the forest know the order of things. They know the Indian must walk his path and the white man his path. That is why our two row wampum belt clearly shows separate paths in the river of life. Our white brother stays in his vessel and we stay in our canoe. The paths never cross, meet each other or touch. The beads never blend together."

"But we're all in the white man's boat. . ."

"Materialistically maybe. Spiritually, I don't think so. I only know you should be true to yourself. Completeness from within is all that really matters." He turned for the door. "I'll wait for you downstairs," he said to Tie. "I want to talk to Jewel's grandpa. I'm sure you two lovebirds won't mind."

Summer ended abruptly and in no time Autumn's falling leaves turned to snowflakes. During the winter months, Tie kept in condition by playing in the Bush Hockey League. Jewel watched him whenever she could but by play off time, her condition prohibited her from going on road trips. She wondered if things could ever be as simple and as clear as Tie's uncle saw them. She guessed not, but her forest experience and his interpretation of it nagged at her mind.

As spring became balmy, the baby became more and more impatient. A compromise between the families had been reached. Instead of a natural child birth in the old way using a midwife, Jewel would go to hospital in the city. Shortly afterwards, Tie's uncle would make arrangements for their traditional marriage. They would exchange their wedding baskets and mating promises on the bank of the river beneath white pine trees.

"I'm glad things have worked out the way they have," Jewel said to Tie as they sat on her front porch. "Not that I'm worried for my own safety, it's just that I want our baby to have the best of everything right from the start." She leaned her head on his shoulder and wrapped herself in his arms. "When next lacrosse season starts, we can move into an apartment in the city."

"That's one of the things I wanted to talk to you about," Tie said. "There's going to be a professional team on the reserve next year. I've been thinking about playing for them."

"Tie, you can't be serious."

"The coach of the team has the school bus contract. He says I can have a job driving one of his buses. That way, we won't have to leave."

Jewel pushed away to look at his eyes. "What about your plans to turn professional with the city team? Didn't they offer you more money?"

Tie leaned forward and put his arms on his knees. "To me, it's *where* the job is that counts."

"I thought this was all settled. You were going to play professional lacrosse in the city. . ."

"We could never live on what I'd make playing in the city. I've been checking rents up there. Even with a subsidy we couldn't make it. . ."

"You could get a part time job."

"Doing what? I'm not educated like you are, you know."

"Yes, I know. Well then, *I'll* get a job. I'm sure I can find something decent."

"No you won't," Tie grabbed Jewel's chin and turned her face toward him. "Coach said he could give me twenty-five dollars a game."

"And when school's out for the summer that's what we live on, eh? Twenty-five dollars a game?"

"Coach said I could wash and repair the buses until fall. We could plant a garden. . ."

Tears streamed down Jewel's cheeks. "What about the baby?" she sobbed. "Maybe you and I could make it but a baby requires additional expenses you know."

"We'll manage."

"Being on subsistence isn't my idea of managing."

"You think that going to the city will solve everything, but it won't. We'll be among strangers; where will we turn? The city's always been your idea but this is where we belong. We have family here."

Jewel jerked his hand away and wiped her eyes. "I guess you're just a backward Indian and you always will be," she said.

"That's right, but I know who I am and I'm not ashamed of it!"

Jewel felt the baby wriggle as she stood up. "I never want to see you again, Titus Joshua." She turned and opened the door. "Never again, EVER!" She slammed the door and one of the panes fell out and broken glass splashed all over the porch.

Two days later, her father drove her to hospital. He tried comforting conversation while her mother sat in quiet gloom. She told Jewel she had telephoned Tie's family to alert them and learned about the breakup at the last minute. She didn't say anything further about the situation except: "What are you going to put on the form that asks the husband's name?"

Jewel replied, "None."

"Don't worry," Jewel's father said. "Baby's come pretty easy in the hospital."

Although the doctor predicted a normal birth, complications arose during delivery and Jewel's baby rested in an incubator for observation. All the other mothers fed their babies daily but Jewel watched her baby through a plastic bubble. She wandered through the ward oblivious to the antiseptic smells and murmurs of visiting husbands. She held her throbbing breasts and believed that her baby was going to die.

On the fourth day, the babies were distributed with their usual ceremony. Jewel hated this time most; she was jealous of the other mothers and usually went for a walk. She slipped on her moccasins but one of the nurses came toward her carrying a pink bundle. Jewel peeked inside and recognized a wrinkled face and a tiny, waving hand. She grabbed for the bundle.

"No, no, my dear," the nurse said. "Climb back into bed first, then I'll give her to you."

Jewel's heart pounded as she scrambled into bed. "Is she okay? Are you sure?"

"She's just fine," the nurse said. "Have you picked out a name for her yet?"

Jewel received the bundle and cradled it. "No."

"You should call her Bright Eyes; she's got the biggest little eyes I've ever seen. Too bad the father skipped out on you. . ."

"What makes you say a thing like that?"

"Well," the nurse sighed. "I couldn't help but notice that your baby's illegitimate and I assumed. . ."

"There's no such thing as an illegitimate child among my people," Jewel snapped.

"Oh." The nurse handed Jewel a baby bottle. "You needn't get uppity about it my dear. These days we deliver quite a few ill---uh, babies to unwed mothers, you needn't be ashamed."

"I'm not ashamed. And I walked out on her father, he didn't walk out on me."

"Of course you did, my dear."

"And I won't be needing your plastic baby bottle, thank you."

"Well," the nurse turned away. "If you need anything else just squeeze the rubber ball behind your head and I'll come running."

Jewel stared at her wide-eyed daughter. For the first time in her life she succumbed to a feeling of pride. She became oblivious to the world around them and gently kissed the baby's forehead.

"You do have bright eyes," she whispered. "Maybe Crystal is your temporary name. Yes, Crystal. At least it'll do until your father and I can get you a proper Onkwehon:we name."

She gave the baby her breast.

The Red Moccasins

Out go two visitors in a swirl of brittle leaves. They'll click pictures beside the Friendship Centre's totem pole and pass through the iron gate out front. Before I started pushing brooms and changing light bulbs, I thought I was passing through myself. Now you may ask, what's a fifty-six year old, intelligent, dude like me doing here? I don't know.

One thing I do know is that you can never tell who's coming through those double-doors next. The first time Derek came through, he hit them with such force you'd have thought they were a tackling dummy. He tripped over my pail and darn near kicked it over. He looked startled, rubbed his shin and cracked a weak smile. "Se:koh," he said, leaping to his feet.

Se:koh is a word we Mohawks greet ourselves with so I let his accident pass without my customary lecture about not running through the hallways. "Sekuli," I said.

From his energetic actions I guessed him to be no more than twenty. His loose black hair hung like fringes over his forehead and a fine, square-shouldered body hinted at athletic prowess. His skin looked like a polished Mocha bean and if he had any outward physical flaw, it was the small space between his front teeth.

"Okwaho ni waka'taro:toh."

"We speak English here," I said flexing my authority. "That way nobody gets offended."

The staccato-like quickness of his speech told me that he came from Kahnawa:ke Reserve. It's said that Mohawks from there get their speed from the rapids of the St. Lawrence River. He said that he's wolf clan which makes us, as the white man inaccurately puts it, blood brothers.

"Is there dance class here today?"

"Dance class? What kind of dance class?"

"My friend told me there was a class here; where they teach you powwow dancing."

"I dunno," I shrugged. I dipped my mop and sloshed it on the floor. "You could ask Mildred; she's the boss. Her office is in the back. . .just go right in. . .she won't hurt you, eh?" I winked and started working my mop.

I never heard of anybody teaching powwow dancing before but who knows? They're always coming up with new things these days. And who would have thought they'd ever permit native languages? Heck-enit, my parents say they got slapped across their hands with rulers if they spoke Mohawk in school. So to protect me, they never taught it; I only learned what I could pick up.

I heard scurrying footsteps behind me and accelerated my mopping stroke. Bosses always walk the quickest and there's no sense letting them catch you going at half speed. I squeezed my face into a smile and turned toward the footsteps.

"She says there's dance class but it isn't for powwow dancing," Derek looked down.

He seemed overly desperate for such a young man. "What kind of class is it?" I frowned to show my concern.

"It's some kind of cultural dancing, but it's modern cultural dancing. Like contemporary-interpretive and stuff like that."

"OhhhHHH-yeah," I said in a singsong fashion I use when I don't understand something. I rinsed my mop.

"Do you know anybody who knows how to fancy dance in powwows?"

I leaned on my mop handle. I pictured a bent, pleasant old man with a billy goat beard and rowdy skin the colour of cardboard. He rests on a cane; his black cowboy hat and boots seem out of place in this Toronto setting. "I think so." I watched Derek's face beam up. "But I'll have to ask around because I'm not sure if he's still in town. Come to think of it, I haven't seen him here for quite awhile."

"You got his phone number?"

"Nah. He wouldn't have no phone. But check back with me in a few days. I gotta get back to work now." I watched him pivot and dodge an elderly lady as he charged out the doorway.

Now I'm not a totally spiritual man but I pay attention to the way things happen. I believe the Creator sends us messages that way. So when Old Fish was the next person to come hobblin' through the doorway, I couldn't help but make the connection. I guessed it my duty to match the old man with the young man; the signal seemed quite clear.

"Se:ko, Old Fish," I said.

"Harrggh-chooo!"

He sneezed so hard he almost knocked himself off his cane. He shuffled his feet to right himself and I noticed his red moccasins. I wondered why he wore them. "Starting to get cold again," I said.

"Yeah!" He leaned on his cane and raised his foot. "Got these new, red moccasins here I wanted you to see. Notice anything different about them?" He pulled one off and handed it to me.

I touched it to my nose and inhaled the clean, fresh scent of smoked, home-tanned moose hide. His new moccasin was decorated with dyed-red porcupine quills and trimmed with home-tanned red fox. A beaded lightning bolt ran down the tongue toward the big toe. "Mighty fine," I winked.

"No, no. What *feels* different about it?"

I squeezed the soft moose hide and wondered what answer the old man expected. "I dunno." I gave it back to him. "I can't feel *any*thing."

"Ha, ha, ha. Of course you can't." He slipped it on.

I pursed my lips and nodded. "You remember telling me about how you used to dance in Buffalo Bill's Wild West Show when you were a kid? Well, I got a kid that wants to learn how to powwow dance. I figure you'd be just the one to teach him, eh. . .?"

The old man raised his eyes and I felt heat bathing my face like a sun lamp.

". . . he's kinda clumsy. I, uh, I dunno what kind of money he can pay. . ."

"You Mohawks are always worrying about money just like the white man, Old Fish snorted. "Never mind 'bout that because it ain't up to me." He shuffled off toward the recreation room. "I'll be here next Friday if he's still interested."

One thing about this job is you learn a lot. For instance, they say Old Fish came from Nevada desert near Walker River. They say when he was a little boy, he met with Wovoka, the Paiute Messiah of the Ghost Dance religion. They say Old Fish got his name because he is a Fish Eater or Paiute. I heard these things over a period of time and have no reason to disbelieve any of them.

Sometimes, I watched Old Fish teaching Derek to dance in the Rec Room. But powwow dancing isn't what went on in there. Old Fish drummed on a gourd that floated around in a galvanized washtub. *Bung-bung-bung* went the drum. Derek's movements imitated a deer's strut with careful, high leg kicks and quick head twists. He pulled his arms in close to his body and bent his hands down like rabbits do when they sit up.

But something didn't look right. Derek just couldn't seem to blend the quick, foot movements with the graceful, upper body

movements. One time, I asked Old Fish how they were making
out. "Brrr," he shrugged.

They practised this way for two months while winter's crispness
slowly advanced. I'd peek in on them once in awhile, make a progress assessment, and go on with my domestic engineering duties.
So when Derek wore Old Fish's red moccasins for the first time, I
noticed it right off. But something didn't seem right.

Sure, Derek lost his clumsiness. And he seemed to have gained
confidence as well. He'd dance smooth as a snow drift for a while
then flail his arms as if struggling to regain his balance. It seemed
like the moccasins were pushing his legs up and pulling them
down. Sort of like the crankshaft driving the pistons instead of
vice versa.

Next time I looked in on them, a small crowd had gathered to
watch. There wasn't any struggling going on now. Derek danced
perfect as a Loon's eerie cry. And Old Fish seemed content; happily beating the gourd in his new Reeboks. He even mumbled a
kind of low, grunting song.

Mildred clued me in about their shows. Somebody's always cal-
ling the Friendship Centre to borrow dancing Indians and she had
scheduled their first few appearances. They danced for church
groups, women groups, schools and Universities. Once she even
invited me to watch them on video tape; a mother proud of her
children. Derek fancy-danced in an explosion of day-glo feathers
and when he kicked up his legs to prance during Crow Hop, I
noticed the red moccasins. By now they had a lot of dancing
mileage on them but looked new as ever.

The next time I saw Derek, he seemed haggard. "Se:koh," he
said.

"Well?" I squeezed out a wink. "How do you like being a
dancer?"

"It's okay." He brushed past me. "I'm making a lot of money and
I'm going to be making a lot more. I'm going on the North Amer-

ican powwow circuit."

The next time I saw Old Fish he was even less cheerful than Derek. It must have been early February because I'd just come back from Mid-winter Longhouse ceremonies back home. Our Mid-winter used to be first moon after the shortest day, December 21st. But because the natural world's disrupted by the white man's Christmas during this time, it's been moved back one moon.

Anyway, Old Fish tapped me on the shoulder one night and darn near sent me to the Great Spirit. I had dozed off in Mildred's comfortable executive chair after checking out the Centre's new budget. I like to see that I'm still in there; not being replaced by some janitorial service. I must have jerked awake because I startled the old man and his eyes bulged out big as those gold, dollar coins.

"Here," he said. He laid a bundle in front of me wrapped in newspaper like you get at the Fish 'n Chips store. "You take this package outside and burn it under a tree. You do this at the next moon."

"OhhhHHH-yeah," I nodded.

"Keep it close to you but don't look inside."

I picked up the package to gauge its weight. I studied it and turned it end to end. It wasn't heavy and it seemed odourless. When I looked up, Old Fish had vanished as ghostly as he had entered.

I never saw Old Fish or Derek after that. They say Old Fish went back to Nevada to die among his people. I heard that Derek planned to stay in town until the start of powwow season, but I never tried to find him. Instead, I did what Old Fish told me.

Snow glowed fluorescent under the mid-March full moon. I wandered around trying to guess what kind of tree would be most appropriate; heck-enit, I never knew they had *any* trees in Nevada. I decided on a spruce but settled on an oak in Queen's Park. Shadows from its branches fell like tangled veins on the snow.

Just as I lit a match, the wind picked up as if huffing to stop my effort. With my last match, I skillfully cupped my hands and lit the package in three places. Thick, black smoked belched from it and the wind stopped. I watched the newspaper start to peel and separate. Fire licked at the package and caused something red inside to fizz and bubble. It showered sparks like a welding torch before it quit.

"Hey! What are you doing there?"

I turned and a flashlight beam blinded me. "Uh, nothing, nothing." I put my hands toward the fire. "I'm just trying to get warm, eh?"

"Well you better put that out and come with me."

I kicked snow on the fire and a white cloud emerged from the hiss. An outline of an eagle slowly threaded its way between oak branches and floated toward the stars. I looked at the officer for his reaction but he didn't seem to see it.

When we reached the police car, I smiled at its driver. I huffed in the officer's face as he stood beside the car to guide me into the back seat. I didn't want them to think I was drunk; pity was my only chance. Anyway, it must have worked because instead of taking me to the lockup they took me to the Friendship Centre. Just goes to show you never know what to expect from the white man.

Nearly everything happened just the way I told you. Oh, maybe that part about the smoke making an eagle outline is a little creative. But then we're still entitled to a few liberties, eh?

And what's wrong with an old man taking somebody under his wing and trying to teach him to dance in the Old Way. I figure it gave Old Fish a little extra time to do what he had to do. As far as the kid goes, heck-enit, I lit that fire for his own good. After all, what kind of champion could he be relying on his moccasins to win for him?

Sometimes A Lonely Business

Twisting, running, Larry Littlecloud burst from cabin number six with uncommon eagerness. The sagging wooden door, its torn screen floating freely along both corner edges, slapped shut behind him, its noise alerting rats occupying the steel garbage bin nearby. His momentum carried him toward the sanitary unit stationed a few yards behind a cluster of bent, wooden tool sheds. The sheds and cabins interrupted smooth rows of apricot trees and stood in a pond of tanned earth resembling a settlement in the wilderness.

Twelve-year-old Larry splashed cold water on his face from a porcelain basin and watched his breath sweep from his nostrils in the cracked, soap-stained mirror. His wrinkled T-shirt and ragged Levi's permitted the cold to bite at his frail body, but excitement and anticipation made him immune.

"I will get a red one," he said aloud, bobbing his head and watching the reflection of his eyes blink mysteriously when crossing the crack. "I will come back from the auction riding my new bicycle just like the big boys at the school." He pushed the door open and, arms outstretched, closed his hands into fists as if practicing handlebar maneuvers.

Larry stopped and began tying the frayed laces of his sneakers just as Jose Miranda stepped from his cabin. Rubbing both eyes with his knuckles, he sat down heavily on the wooden packing crate that served as a step. "I'm not going today," he said quietly. "My Papa says we need the money for other things." He slumped forward dropping his arms on his thighs and turned reddened eyes toward Larry. "Are you still going?" he asked.

Reluctantly, Larry nodded. He felt a few degrees of captured joy seep from his pounding heart over the sudden emptiness of his friend's news. He noticed his mother's silhouette from the dimly lit window of the adjacent cabin and carefully pulled the lace into a bow. "They're up now," he said. "Guess I'll be going pretty soon."

"You are lucky," Jose said. "You are very lucky."

Larry entered a small kitchen and watched his mother preparing breakfast. A dim, bared light bulb hung by a cloth cord from an exposed beam adding mystery to the room's unfinished corners and giving her quick motions over the two-burner hot plate an eerie effect. Using brighter, more powerful bulbs was frowned upon by the grower and Mr. Littlecloud respected authority with religious sanctity. Larry heard the hiss of cakes in the iron frying pan and smelled the scent of corn.

Mary entered the room through the drapery that was the bedroom door and yawned. Her sleepy button eyes looked at Larry and she turned and talked back toward the cloth: "Papa?" she asked. "Can I go with Larry today?"

A wiry man a head taller than Larry pushed the cloth aside and emerged into the kitchen. His black, shoulder-length hair was streaked with white and a red headband partially covered the tops of thick eye brows. Reservation life had hardened and prematurely aged him, yet mysteriously had failed to blacken his spirit. He placed a hand on Mary's head and stroked his knobby, calloused fingers through her long, ebony hair. "No, Mary," he said firmly.

"Today Larry is to do the work of a man."

Larry's stomach pressed its walls together, the noise sounding like a muffled croak. His gleaming, puppy dog eyes widened proudly at his fathers's remark and he scampered atop the coarse, wooden bench carefully retrieving four plates and forks from a horizontal stud over the table. But it was as if a new understanding of importance gripped him. Certainly he had longed for and even rehearsed the arrival of this day many times, yet a thread of fear began pulsing in his spinal column. The full meaning of his father's words was now becoming burdensome and he began to feel the weakness of uncertainty.

Mama moved toward the head of the gray picnic table which was once used in the grower's yard but now stood duty inside the cabin. Massive nails secured it to the uneven pine plankings of the floor. She held the frying pan like a collection basket in church, her thinness being hidden by the long-pleated, oversize dress donated by Catholic parishioners. Her eyes had become worn and heavy, and the luster that projected from them only a few years ago had rapidly subsided to cloudiness. The last time she laughed, or even smiled, had melted from Larry's memory. But she was a proud woman despite the slowness of her eyes. "I see Papa has no trouble getting you up today," she said.

Mary sat next to Larry, and Mama placed the big, blackened frying pan across the table in front of Papa. During the blessing, Mary presented her finest example of toothless intimidation hoping for a reprieve in Papa's decision, but to no avail. Larry gulped down his cakes and patiently waited for the others to finish. At last Papa stood up and reached deep into his pocket, the darkness of his arm submerging to almost its elbow. "Here is the money," he said, handing Larry a five-dollar bill.

Larry hesitated. "I think you should know that Jose won't be coming," he said.

Papa motioned the money toward Larry. "Perhaps then it is

willed that you must do this thing alone. Being a man is sometimes a lonely business."

"Thank you," Larry said. He took the money, bolted toward the
door and stopped at the pail that stood atop an overturned orange
crate. Water dribbled from the sides of his mouth in silver rivulets
as he gulped it from the tin dipper. "Goodbye Mama, goodbye
Mary," he said.

They answered him in unison and Papa walked out of the cabin
placing his arm firmly around the boy's shoulders. "Be careful on
the road and don't just buy for the sake of buying. Make sure you
get the one you want." He gave an affectionate squeeze and
watched Larry walk briskly beside the crown of dirt rising from
the driveway.

By the time Larry approached the California Highway Patrol
barracks, the sun had been victorious over the morning haze, cast-
ing a brilliance that made him squint. He entered the large asphalt
parking lot and saw a row of bicycles all numbered with a pink
cardboard tag twisted to the handlebars with piano wire. They
stood evenly spaced on their kickstands. A big truck backed up
and two men in denim work suits began unloading more bicycles.

A steady steam of people filtered into the parking lot and began
inspection. Some carried little spring-bound notebooks, jotting
down the numbers of their favorites. Children pressed light and
horn buttons, tested the strength of fenders and kickstands,
kicked at tires and climbed aboard seats with uncanny expertise.

Larry's eyes were immediately attracted to Number 123, a beautiful red Stingray with a wire basket on its handlebars and a
chromium carrier over the rear fender. He pressed at its white-
wall tires and, judging by tread depth, guessed it was almost
brand new. He was unable to find a scratch, dent or rust bubble.
He pictured himself pumping home and the happy curve that would
grace his father's lips over the wisdom of his choice. He overheard

a man command his wife to mark down Number 123 on her pad. She obeyed.

Larry found three more bicycles he liked while a large, flatbed truck loaded with more bicycles crept into the parking lot. He decided to commit his favorites to memory in order of importance: 123, 147, 96 and 78. A wave of people quickly engulfed the truck, pushing for position and enlarging their growing lists of numbers as each bicycle was unloaded. By now a huge crowd had gathered, but the people dissolved from Larry's mind and he saw only the rounded forms of the bicycles.

Finally the truck was barren and a Highway Patrol officer climbed atop its steel-ribbed bed, his badge glinting reflections from the sun. "May I have your attention. Thank you. In accordance with Section. . ."

Larry decided to make certain the Stingray hadn't been changed to a different number. He pushed his way toward it, oblivious to the people who were still busy inspecting the collection that now completely framed the parking lot. There were Stingrays, English racers, old bicycles, new ones, and even a few broken ones of every manufacture, size, color and style. It was a fantasy only a child could truly appreciate. When he found his red favorite, he sighed happily, noting Number 123 remained unchanged.

". . .by the State of California, in and for the County of Santa Clara. All sales are final and there can be no guarantees or refunds. Now this isn't a professional auction," the officer continued, "so let's not have any fancy gesturing or hand waves. Just shout out your bid and the highest one takes it. There's enough bikes here for everybody and we have to get rid of them all. We do ask that you start with a reasonable bid."

"Can parents bid for their children?" a lady shouted.

The officer nodded and the crowd began to buzz in anticipation. One of the Levi-jacketed workmen placed a blue bicycle on the truck bed and the officer held up his hands, palms outward, un-

til the noise subsided. "Okay," he said. "We've got a Huffy. . .looks
like it's in pretty good shape. . .I see one dent in the front fender
but its tires look pretty good. . .Number 17. Who wants to start the
bidding?"

A nervous silence settled over the crowd.

"Okay then, I'll start the bidding," the officer smiled. "Who will
give one dollar? Anybody?" His eyes scanned corner to corner,
hoping to find a bidder. "Come on now. Certainly this fine bike's
worth a dollar to somebody."

"One dollar and thirty cents," a lady in the front row said.

"One thirty-five," blurted a man.

The officer waved his arms. "Hold it, hold it," he said. "I should
have told you that we'll raise the bidding by denominations of
fifty cents only. We've got an awful lot of bikes to get rid of and I
don't want to be here all day."

The woman quickly changed her bid. "One dollar and fifty
cents," she said in a raised voice.

"Two dollars!"

"Two-fifty," shouted a man.

"Ten dollars," yelled a man in bib overalls. His head was slightly cocked and he wavered where he stood.

"Now folks, this is only the first bicycle," the officer said.
"There's plenty more. It might be better to keep the bidding a
little more conservative. Now, sir, do you want to take back your
bid?"

The man swayed slightly, his rubberized neck swivelling its dis-
approval.

"Okay. Sold for ten dollars. Pay the man cash over at the table
there. No checks please."

Two of the numbers Larry had intended to bid on, 96 and 78,
were disposed of in the first hour. The green one sold for twenty-
five dollars, the blue one for sixteen. Larry hadn't managed a bid.

"Okay now folks, here's a real nice one. . .looks brand new. . .a

Schwinn Stingray Number 123. . ."

"Ten dollars!" interrupted a man.

"Fifteen."

"Twenty-five," a well-dressed man in a worsted suit said loudly.

"Thirty," said a lady.

A large, muscular black man wearing a black beret and thick-rimmed solar glasses grunted with displeasure, his face contorting as if in sharp pain.

"Ain't you gonna bid on it?" his wife asked. "That's the one you wanted."

"Hell, I ain't had but one chance to open my mouth all day."

"Thirty-five!" the well-dressed man shouted.

"Forty!"

"Damn," the black man said. "These people are crazy. Man, you can buy a *new* bike for less than that. Come on woman, let's go home. I thought we'd find a bargain here but these cats all lost their cool."

". . .going once, going twice, SOLD for forty-five dollars!"

Larry watched the well-dressed man in the worsted suit pay the officer at the table, take possession of the Stingray and push it through the crowd, one hand behind the banana seat, the other grasping the flecked handle grips. He went to the 'reserved' area behind the barracks and overlapped it atop another red bike in the huge trunk of his Cadillac. He secured the trunk lid with clothesline cord, started his car and disappeared in a surge of power.

Larry walked slowly back to his position, gently squeezing among the crowd. The sun was beginning its descent and a major-ity of the people had grown hostile toward the high bidding. "I thought this auction was for the kids," a man shouted in disgust.

A woman complained: "Yeah! Let the kids do the bidding!"

"Okay. This next bicycle will be bid on by kids only. Adults kindly refrain from bidding." The officer extended his arms in a gathering motion. "Kids, move down in front so's I can hear you."

The gold bicycle that he now held, Number 147, was the sole re-
mainder of the numerals Larry had memorized and was his second
choice.

"Two dollars!" a young voice bellowed.

"Four!"

"Fifteen cents," a little boy shouted, the pitch of his soprano
voice sounding like the amplified squeak of a microphone. The
crowed roared its endorsement and Larry's bid of five dollars
wasn't heard.

"Sold to the boy in the red plaid shirt for fifteen cents," the
officer shouted. The crowd applauded heartily and the little boy
smiled in bashful triumph.

Children bid on more bicycles that day, but Larry didn't participate, for he had begun the eternal four-mile journey home. A
chill began surging inside him and he broke into a trot to keep
warm. He pushed his wrists against the moisture forming in his
eyes but he didn't weep. The movements of his legs were numb
and automatic, and when he reached the familiar surroundings of
the orchards, little crusts of soft earth invaded his torn sneakers
unnoticed. His eyes focused on the cabins and he rested, listening
to the tunes of the curled leaves rustling above him.

Then, reluctantly, he followed tire tracks toward his cabin, his
heart pounding like ceremonial drums. He thought of his father
and of the improved living conditions since leaving the Reservation. Suddenly his ears became filled with the chant of wisdom.
But when the screen door rapped closed behind him, the noise was
like an explosion in Larry's ears and awakened him to reality.

"Did you get a bicycle?" Mama asked.

"No," Larry said, his heavy eyes sinking to the floor. He cleared
his throat and swallowed. "They were all old. . .most of them had
broken gears and everything."

"Were there lots of bicycles there?"

"Yes. But they were all old and broken."

Larry's mother stared at him. He was standing as if frozen, his eyes magnetized to an uneven plank in the floor. Slowly her taut, horizontal lips moved into an upward curl. "Maybe it's just as well," she said in a proud tone. "You need a new pair of sneakers anyways, don't you?"

"Yes, Mama," Larry said.

Reunion

To get there, from the multi-level concrete parking lot, you climb patio brick stairs to the street. Across the busy thoroughfare, through thick glass doors, is the entrance to a multi-level shopping mall named Farmer's Square. This is the core of the city. One must try to visualize a farmer's market on this spot. That's what used to be here and is the reason my people relinquished this parcel; to allow natural commerce to flourish. When the farmers were expelled and use outside the agreement began, it's said that a curse of ill fortune was cast upon it. Yet I feel no discomfort with the past. On this hot, sticky day, humidity is my only discomfort.

Having just entered the mall, air conditioning is a delicious relief. I remove my sunglasses and they dangle from their cord bouncing against my chest as I march toward Easton's Department Store. I'm shopping for one of those little plastic boxes that hold cassette tapes. I wouldn't have come here except nobody else in town has a match for the others I have; at thirty-nine, I've become a stickler for detail. There's no directory at the entrance; I'll have to ask for directions.

I proceed through Women's Apparel amid racks and counters and mannequins draped in assortments of the latest fashion. Ladies representing every adjective hold selections to their bosoms gazing hopefully at panels of mirrors. If anybody can direct me it'll be one of these seasoned veterans. She's mashing hangers together at a circular rack below a MINISKIRTS 20% OFF! sign. I wonder what the full length of a miniskirt is. Her denim shorts are frayed; veins in her thighs have exploded into a pattern of spider webs. Maybe a maxi dress would be more suitable.

"Miss? Can you tell me where I can find some little plastic boxes?"

She looks at me as if deciding the purity of my intentions. "I'm sorry," she shrugs. "You'll have to find a saleslady---I don't work here." She pivots and walks briskly away.

Suddenly, a lovely young woman I guess to be twenty-ish walks toward me. Beaded, eagle feather earrings peek through strands of her long hair whose blackness gives a nice contrast to her short, fluorescent green dress. She squints her brown eyes as if searching for something. As she comes closer, they begin questioning me. I guess that she's an Indian girl but that's not what's drawing my attention. She seems familiar. Just as I'm about to speak, she beams me out and walks past me.

I veer toward a candy counter. "Which way to where they sell plastic boxes?" I ask an antiseptic clerk.

"Over by the escalator," she says. "Straight ahead until you come to Yarns, turn right until you get to Pots and Pans and then down three aisles on your right."

I'm not paying any attention; my mind is obsessed with identifying the girl in the fluorescent mini-dress. I know I've seen those big, questioning, brown eyes before. I stretch my neck to watch her lifting blouses from a long sales counter. She discards two of them and quickly walks toward Casuals with her hair adrift. To her almost too large hips, the fluorescent dress clings. Her matching high-heeled shoes give her the bouncy, authoritative walk of a fashion model. I'm sure I know her.

"Excuse me please, I'd like to see those slacks," a squeaky voice from behind me says.

"Oh, of course," I say, stumbling toward the check-out counter.

The girl impatiently drums her fingernails, looks at me and forces a smile. Now that I've caught a close up, I'm positive I know her. But from where? Her flat, kitten-like face and bold movements are definitely familiar. Yet my mind pictures her wearing a brown business suit---it's her clothes that are wrong!

Something tugs at my arm. An old lady, eighty-ish, with silver chains attached to her thick bifocals loudly asks, "Young man. Do you have any white binders?"

"What?"

"White binders," she talks very slowly. "White, three ringed binders like the kids use in school."

"I don't know," I say with great emphasis in case she can't see me. "I don't work here."

"Oh," she smiles. "How about blue. You got any blue ones?"

"I. . .don't. . .work. . .here."

"Never mind. I don't want yellow. Thank you anyway."

I turn back toward the girl but it's too late. She's gone. I skim the entire area. I rush toward Shoes, pass the escalator, see an assortment of cassette tape boxes but head for the exit. I notice one of the side doors closing; somebody's just left.

I burst outside and the brilliant sun makes me put my sunglasses on but I see nothing fluorescent green. I skip across the street and look inside a cafe window. Shielding my eyes from window reflections, I become aware that something else seems to be pushing me to go inside.

I quickly check and reject women whose bodies are concealed behind high-backed booths. This place is right out of the 50's with its chromium-trimmed furniture and Select-O-Matic jukebox. I decide on coffee to soothe my defeated spirit and push a plastic tray along a stainless steel shelf, past glass cases of leafy salads and

cooked foods. I pay the cashier, check the dining area for fluorescent green and sit at a centrally located table. Movement of two
new women attracts my attention but it seems hopeless. Gazing at
the reflection of the ceiling fan on the shiny table top, the memory
that's been so elusive suddenly erupts with volcanic force; sweeping me up in its lava flow to another place. . .

I had left the rez that Friday to take Lloyd Faber, the friend I had
always been most comfortable with during Brantford Collegiate
days, for a ride in my new, six-year old, 1964 Rambler. We had
both grown up fatherless and had stumbled through adolescence
together sharing life's intimate findings and comparing notes.
Though he had moved away to Hamilton shortly after graduation,
his mother always felt it her duty to keep me informed of all his
latest news.

Parking in a wide, graveled driveway beside Lloyd's apartment
house, I squinted into the afternoon sun and saw his lanky silhouette swinging toward a furry lump at the end of an oak branch. A
kids gathering had turned his spectacle into an entertainment but
his lady, Janice, stood with palms on cheeks in open-mouthed in-
tensity. The ca-chunk of my closing car door caused everybody to
look my way and that's when I saw the young woman for the first
time. Then twenty and though still numb with youth, I felt something twinkle inside.

"Tum on, tum on, Ringlet," Lloyd said in baby talk. He hung by
one hand, peeled a banana with his teeth and voiced his invitation
between stokes. "Tum to Da-da like a good liddle boy."

Ringlet, a spider monkey with a long tail stared at Lloyd and
nervously worked his miniature hands. He showed his teeth and
backed safely out of reach. "*Ch-ch-ch-ch-ch-ch,*" he said. His
plastic-like face and beady eyes emitted an air of superiority.

Lloyd extended the peeled banana. "Tum on," he said.

I brushed off my Levi's and approached the group like Joe Cool,
I was proud to finally have a car. The girl cradled a kitten, her

black hair covered it like a satin sheet. She smiled at me, kissed
the top of the kitten's head and looked up at the tree.

Ten feet above the ground Lloyd saw me. "Hey Wayne," he
hollered. "What are *you* doing here?"

"I came to watch you fall on your head---"

"Now you be careful, Honey," Janice said. "Maybe if you took
the kitten up there with you Ringlet'd come down."

"Hell no," Lloyd said. "Then I'd have both of them to worry
about. I'll be down in a minute, Wayne."

Lloyd played piano and had taken a five-piece jazz group to
Toronto to audition for an American theatrical agency. They were
scheduled to play the 'B' tour, which began in Montreal complete
with new singer, new name and new rock and roll arrangements.
Six months ago they had stopped for a visit and I met Janice. That
was the last time I'd seen or heard of them until his mother called,
gave me this address and told me Lloyd's group had a gig in
Hamilton.

"Don't go out on that limb any further," Janice said. "It'll break
off and you'll fall on your ass. Give me that kitten." She grabbed it
from the girl. "Come down here Ringlet!" She thrust the kitten
upward. Held firmly around its belly, the kitten mewed and
twirled its legs attempting balance. "You get down here this minute and play with Midnight!" She stepped closer to the tree leaving the girl to my curious eyes.

At the hips, the miniskirt of a business woman's suit clung;
smooth curves were enhanced by the sunlight. Brown high heels,
matching handbag and white gloves made me think of a fashion
magazine, yet her ingenue quality suggested she was my age. She
looked at me and fluffed her hair.

"Hi," I said, noticing her high cheekbones.

"I'm Lloyd's friend," she said as if my stare demanded explanation.

A groaning sound drew attention to the tree. Accompanied by a loud snap, Lloyd and Ringlet fell to the ground. At the moment of impact, Ringlet somersaulted like a circus tumbler and raced into Janice's outstretched arms. Lloyd stood up, rubbed his hip and licked squashed banana meat off his fingers. When he finally smiled to indicate survival, everybody burst out laughing.

"You needn't have hurried," I told him.

"Are you all right, Honey?" Janice asked, then she added "poor baby," while looking at Ringlet so you weren't sure whom she addressed.

"Yeah," Lloyd said. "I could've broken a finger or something."

Outwardly, his appearance was ruinous. His eye for proper grooming always betrayed him; his clothes hung rather than fit. Squared shoulders, thin waist and awkward movements brought a klutz to mind but when seated behind a piano, ice couldn't be smoother. His world of clefs and notes superseded everything else and whatever his eyes lacked in taste, his ears made up for: he was gifted with perfect pitch.

"Let's go upstairs and have a beer," he said. "You kids'll have to go now."

We shook hands and climbed the outside back stairs single file. I wanted to mention my new car but the timing seemed inappropriate. Squeezing tight when the girl lifted herself up, her skirt revealed undergarment markings which traced the arcs of her buttocks. "Pretty nice, eh?" I said to Lloyd though not exactly sure why this daring observation had escaped.

We entered the doorway and a malodorous paint smell engulfed us. A rounded refrigerator, pitted dinette, and four vinyl chairs, exposing yellow cotton from their wounds, were in the centre of the kitchen.

"We're furnishing in early Salvation Army," was Janice's explanation. She put Ringlet in an upright cage that stood near the sink. She lowered the kitten to the floor beside a saucer whose curdled milk scribbled a shoreline. "Lloyd," she said. "Hand me the bottle of milk."

Lloyd looked inside the refrigerator. "There's no more milk; he'll have to drink beer."

"Oh, Lloyd. You know beer makes him tipsy."

"It does too," Lloyd said to me. "We got them both drunk one night---you should have seen them." He laughed while placing two glasses and four bottles of O'Keefe's on the table. "Oh," he said. "This is Susie Peters. Susie, this is Wayne Isaiah. Wayne's an old chum of mine; you might say we grew up together, eh Wayne?"

I nodded in unison with gulping my beer in an attempt at coolness.

Susie sat across from me and removed her gloves. She placed them between handle loops of her purse, kicked off her shoes and folded her legs up. Lloyd straddled his chair and sat down while Janice poured Susie's beer.

"You might say Susie's a friend of ours, isn't that right Honey?," Janice said, in a catty tone.

"She's a fashion model at the Royal Connaught where all the big executives go for private showings. She shows the latest evening wear from New York and Paris."

"Tell him how much that one gown cost," Janice said to Susie. "Was it thirteen hundred or fifteen hundred?"

"Thirteen hundred." Susie stared into her glass as if embarrassed.

Lloyd said, "She's a good singer too; sounds a little like Joan Baez. I'm working up an arrangement for her right now. . ."

I looked at Susie and Lloyd's conversation shut off. I thought about the glamour of her occupation and guessed at the number of men she must be dating. Though being a fashion model enhanced her status, it put a great distance between us. Yet when she smiled at me, I detected a slight trace of vulnerability.

". . .it'll be a sexy number, the kind of thing Roberta Flack does."

"What songs do you sing?" I asked her.

"Lloyd's working up a jazz arrangement of Summertime for me," she said softly.

"Yeah. It'll be *real* sexy," Lloyd laughed.

"It's the arrangement that makes the song, but I'm not trying to become a vocalist. I don't care about seeing my name up in lights. It's just something I've always wanted to do."

"Speaking about *seeing* things," Janice interrupted. "Have you seen your daughter lately?" She took a sip of beer, held a cigarette to her lips and glared at Lloyd. "How about a light?"

Susie's eyes dropped and disappeared behind a hairy hand reaching across in front of me holding a flickering Ronson. I must have misheard the question; this must be some sort of cruel joke. I took a big gulp of beer and felt a splash of foam hit my upper lip. Could she really have a kid?

"Yes." Susie raised her eyes. "I went over to my mother's house last Wednesday---"

"You should see her," Janice said. "She's the cutest thing---looks just like her mother." She snapped her fingers and held them to her temple. "What's her name? I'm afraid I've forgotten."

"Julia."

"How old is she now? Three? Four?"

"Julia's two and a half."

Lloyd finished his beer. He thumped his bottle on the table and pushed his chair out. "Come on, Wayne," he said. "We'll let these women gab about kids and monkeys and kittens but I want to show you a man's toy."

Following him down a hallway, I peered inside a vacant room and recognized his battered, portable phonograph. A shadeless lamp and strewn records, resembling stepping stones, were the only things kept here. When we got to his bedroom, he fumbled through two dresser drawers before ending his search with a smile of satisfaction. I expected him to pitch me a bag of marijuana; I remembered the previous year when he had first discovered what he called musician's medicine. Instead, he pulled out a snub-nosed revolver and twirled it around his finger, cowboy fashion. He tossed it to me.

"Where did you get *this*?" I asked.

Lloyd grinned. "I wear it to work in my shoulder holster. All of us carry one since we got beat-up by some drunken punks in Montreal." He took it from me and laughed. "It's not real; it's a blank gun. But you'd be surprised how much peace of mind you get---especially in the bars we have to play in." He wheeled toward the dresser mirror, crouched and pretended to fan the hammer. "Fabulous Faber, champion of the people," he said.

"Lloyd, Honey." Janice yelled. "Why don't you go to the store and get some milk? Susie says she'll stay for supper so you'd better pick up some steak and butter. Ask Wayne if he'll stay."

"He's staying," yelled Lloyd.

We drove to a supermarket and Lloyd rambled on about his romantic exploits like a bragging sailor. He said the band had a communal Cadillac the sax player was using and that a Montreal affair with an older French woman had liberated him from his Victorian sexual ideas. He confided that Janice wasn't legally his wife, her Catholic husband wouldn't allow divorce, yet he savoured their relationship and seemed happy in his situation. I let him drive back to the apartment and he ground the Rambler's gears twice explaining that he had become accustomed to automatic shifting.

"How do you like her?" he asked.

"Fine, just fine," I said. "I almost bought a Chev but decided---"

"Not the car, stupid, Susie! How do you like her?"

"She's okay, I guess."

"Come on Wayne. Quit trying to be cool. She's a real doll; I think she's Mohawk like you, eh? But watch out---she's kind of spacy."

"Spacy?"

"She stares off sometimes as if she's somewhere else. She must be kind of screwed up or something; she takes medication pills. Funny thing about women. The more beautiful they are the more head-funny they seem to be."

"What about her husband? She *does* have one doesn't she?"

"Yeah," Lloyd sighed. "He's real jealous of her too. I met him one morning when he came over to the apartment. We had just finished a gig over at the club and Janice and I were having something to eat. He damn near broke our door down because he thought we lied to him about Susie's whereabouts. If it hadn't been for Susie, I'd of called the cops and had him thrown in jail."

"He must be a real punk," I said, suddenly infuriated about Susie's predicament. "No wonder she's spacy.

"Susie says she's through with him but you can never be sure. They always end up going back to their husbands. But play your cards right and who knows? You could end up with a model chalked up on your coup stick. Ha, ha, ha."

At the apartment, it didn't take the women much time to prepare dinner. For most of the meal, Janice and Lloyd related their road experiences as if engaged in play acting. Janice would proceed to an anticlimactic place and then relinquish the conversation to Lloyd. Susie nibbled at her food and occasionally nodded and looked at me and smiled. She was the enchantment I had perceived a thousand times, I had personally assembled her cell by cell and it seemed a miracle that she existed.

Afterward, Janice pushed dirty dishes to the centre of the table and we sat, discussing. Lloyd carried on about who the current jazz musicians were and which ones were superior instrumentalists. Susie sipped at her coffee, its curtain of steam seemed to make her eyes blurry. Without explanation, she rose from her chair and disappeared into the hallway. Lloyd announced his intention to change his clothes and after Janice followed him, I decided to find Susie.

I peeked inside an empty room and saw her standing by a paint-spattered window. She was scraping at paint runs with her long fingernails and staring off into space. She turned and her eyes seemed troubled and confused and a single tear slalomed down her cheek. I went to her and her eyes filled with water and she laid her head on my chest.

My arms encircled her, drew her in and she fit snug as a puzzle piece. When I felt her body relax, I gently kissed her temple. I wanted to tell her things of poetry, of beauty, of love, but we were too new to each other; not even friends. "What's wrong," I whispered, "Don't say anything," she answered and we stood quietly contemplating.

She looked up at me, her doe eyes beckoning. Our lips met, and lust forced our mouths to open and my passion exploded into thousands of spinning crystals. We remained locked, our heads tipping and rolling, our breaths exchanged, spinning, our tongues flicking messages and suddenly she pushed me away.

"Oh, Susie," I gasped. My mind struggled at explanation, blood rushed through my bowels like the down-sweep of a roller coaster. What's wrong with her? Doesn't she know? Is she stupid? In desperation I put my hand on her shoulder. "It's your husband," I said finally. "You've found out you really love him after all," was my immediate conclusion.

Two swelled tears covered her eyes. "That's not it," she said softly. "I've never loved him, never, NEVER!" Her lashes blinked and two droplets were dispatched. "I've always felt sorry for him. He's like a little boy with a prized lollipop and soon he won't have it anymore. . ."

Her fatigued face suddenly brightened as if some inner register had rung up a total. Her eyes glowed like filaments and she rested her damp cheek against my shoulder. She pulled my arms about her like a child wrapping itself in a blanket. I felt her body grow limp and kissed her temple. I continued down her cheek and neck and she raised her chin and I kissed the hollow between her clavicles and moved into the valley between her breasts.

"You shouldn't," she whispered. "You can't---it wouldn't be fair to you, no, No, NO!" She pushed me away. "You *can't* be my lover."

"What's wrong. Have I done something wrong?"

"No," she cried. "It's not you, it's *me*."

At that instant, booming voices flooded the air, Janice's shriek suggesting danger. From the kitchen, a coarse voice bellowed accusations and I heard Lloyd answer them with a threat. Curse words were exchanged and Susie rushed toward the door wiping away tears with her wrists. I followed her into the kitchen.

"She's not here---now get the hell out!" Lloyd yelled.

A short, blond headed broad-shouldered man stood inside the doorway. When he saw Susie, his eyes became slits as he thrust himself forward. With the sweep of an arm, he pushed the dishes off the table, their loud crash caused Ringlet to begin scolding. Lloyd, naked except for his undershorts, moved toward the intruder with fists clenched. Janice, clutched her bathrobe closed, it had no belt to hold her inside.

"This's Herby---Susie's nutty husband," Lloyd said to me. "And for breaking my dishes, I'm going to break his head."

As I glared at the man bent over the table, energies of hatred at his mistreatment of Susie built. With Lloyd at the other side of the table, the intruder's eyes darted back and forth as we moved toward him. He saw me clench my fists and he started whining. His cheeks puffed up and veins in his neck reached pencil thickness. He emitted a low, gurgling sound, picked up a steak knife and began slashing the air in front us.

"Oh, God, no," Janice screamed. "I can't watch this." She turned and ran down the hallway.

Suddenly, he lunged at me and I jumped backward crashing against the refrigerator. As I struggled for balance, Susie raced between us. "Stop it Herby! Stop it!" she shouted.

He pushed her aside and stumbled backward. He squeezed his face in anger, issued an animal growl and slashed at the air. Lloyd and I stood motionless when Janice swept into the kitchen and tossed Lloyd the revolver. He clicked back its hammer, stiffened his arm and aimed at Herby's head.

Herby bellowed a ghastly sound. Like a wounded animal, he dropped the knife and staggered out the doorway. Susie's face mirrored a reaction that was neither condemning, hateful, nor loving. She put on her shoes, pulled on her gloves, picked up her purse and walked toward the door. Before she left she faced me and I read disappointment in her eyes and she was gone.

"They always go back to their husbands," Lloyd said.

I never saw much of them after that; they went south and now that I had wheels, I decided to give iron working a try. My pride wouldn't allow search of Susie, no, it was *she* who had turned her back on *me*. Lloyd's group played backup for a singer who had one hit record and now, sitting alone in this cafe, I can only wonder at what might have nullified his musical success.

I put my cup down, push out the chair and start for the exit. Through the window a fluorescent green reflection glints. I trace its hypotenuse to a booth beside a panelled wall. A girl in a green fluorescent dress stabs a fork at a piece of lettuce, purse and parcels strewn beside her. Head tilted downward, her long, black hair curtains her face as I approach.

I hover over her and she looks up at me, her small munches quick as a rabbit's. Her brown eyes dance with innocence yet demand explanation. She swallows.

"Would you like some?" she asks.

A mental picture of Susie overlays her face and fuses perfectly except for cosmetic colouring. Amazed at this illusion, I feel my mouth open.

"Are you sure you don't want any, Mister?"

"Uh, no, no. I, I just had a cup of coffee over there." I point over there. "Do you mind if I sit down?" I sit down. "I saw you over in Easton's---"

She chooses another piece of lettuce. "No," she smiles. "I saw *you* in Easton's. Let's get our facts straight, eh?"

"Okay, okay, you saw *me* in Easton's. That's what I want to talk to you about."

"Easton's?"

"No facts. You see there's someth---"

In a concerned voice she asks, "Are you the fuzz?" She continues her munching.

"No, I'm not the fuzz."

"Whew," she says. "The way you've been following me around I thought you were." She moves her eyes and head from side to side as if she's going to divulge an atomic secret. "You see, I steal things," she whispers. Wiping her mouth with a napkin, she looks at me and bursts out laughing. "Not really. . ."

"Do you always put people on?"

"Only when they interrupt me in the middle of my lunch."

"Are you a fashion model?" I blurt out.

She stabs another piece of lettuce and holds it up to her mouth, the dressing dripping into the bowl. "Don't tell me," she says. "Let me guess. You want to teach me how to table dance so's I can make $200,000 a year because you can't find any Native girls to do it. Only there's one slight catch, right."

"No, no," I say. "My name's Wayne Isaiah. I'm from Six Nations."

"Six Nations? You know Chip Isaiah, used to play lacrosse?"

". . .used to play goalie for the Wolves?"

She nods. "He also *used* to be my boyfriend." She puts the lettuce in her mouth but her eyes have taken on curiosity's sparkle. Her tongue sweeps over her lips cleaning smudges of dressing.

"Is your name Julia? Julia Peters?"

"What do you know about Julia Peters?"

"Almost nothing. You see it was her mother that I knew."

She puts the fork down and pats her mouth with a napkin. "Well," she sighs. "You're half right. My name is Julia, but it's Julia Samson, not Peters." She pushes her chair out.

"Is your mother Susie---Susie Peters?"

Her face emits a ghostlike glow. "Bingo," she says. "My mother's name was Susie Peters. Why?"

"Well I knew your mother when she modeled in Hamilton. You were probably too little to remember. . ."

"I know she was a model."

". . .and now little Julia's all grown up and married."

"Married?" She stands and gathers her packages. "I'm *not* married."

"Well how did you get the name Samson?"

"I was brought up by my grandparents. After mum died they had my name legally changed---"

"Died? Did you say your mother died?"

"Yes. She died when I was two and a half years old."

"She died. . ."

"Yeah. She had diabetes and for the longest time my grandparents---hey, what's wrong? Are you all right?"

"Uh, yeah, yeah, I'm okay. . ."

"I don't know what happened to my Dad after that; I never saw him. Grandpa retired and we moved back to the reserve. Now I live here, in town."

She pivots and strides toward the door with vigour and vanishes as quickly as her mother did. I stand and walk toward the door feeling empty inside, the torment in Susie's eyes of disappointment branded in my memory forever.

When I cross the street, a blast of hot air hits me in the face but I purposely avoid going back inside Farmer's Square on my way to the car.

The Smooth Water Pilgrimage

When Peter John floor-boarded the gas pedal, his car coughed, sputtered, backfired and died. As it rolled to a stop, he took his Grandfather's medicine pouch from the passenger's seat and looped it around his neck. The pouch, detailed instructions and a relieved look were the last things he remembered about his Grandfather's death bed. Peter wondered why Tota chose him for this errand; at seventeen he was too young to understand the wisdom of his elders.

He stuffed a pair of pliers into the hip pocket of his jeans, pushed the car off the road and set fire to it. Burnt vehicles disintegrated faster and as a precaution against future enemy use, were routinely destroyed. Though Peter didn't think the white skins would be this far north with fall approaching, you could never be sure of anything during wartime.

Using the morning sun as a directional tool, he determined cross country would be his quickest route to the Longhouse. Tota warned him that Grand Council would be in session when he arrived but the tobacco in his pouch would be welcomed. Fringe from his buckskin vest tickled his chest in cadence with his jogging stride.

From the top of a hill, he saw an old, gasoline powered yellow school bus creating a rooster tail of dust on a gravelled road. Soul Brothers was scribbled in purple paint beneath its black side-stripe. Peter increased his pace; if he hurried he could intersect the bus and bargain for a ride.

A barbed wire fence blocked his path and he snipped it with the pliers and smiled. White skins had once imprisoned the land but that would be ending soon. Nobody can own Mother Earth just as nobody but Sonkwaiatis:on can own the clouds or the sun.

He waved his arms and the bus hissed to a stop. Three rifle barrels and a pistol pointed at him from darkened windows.

"I'm not a white skin," Peter yelled. "I'm onkwehon:we! Kanienkeha:ka. . .Mohawk." He raised his arms and held the medicine pouch above his head. "I'm peaceful. I need a lift to Grand Council."

A black man wearing a purple beret hopped from the bus dressed in battle fatigues; a holstered Colt .45 dangled from his hip. A gold ring pierced an earlobe and a flash of sunlight reflected from his steel rimmed sunglasses.

"What's your name?" he asked. He puffed on a cigar, exhaled smoke from the side of his mouth and waved Peter forward. Simultaneously, the gun barrels pulled back inside the bus. "Man, what's your name?"

"Peter John."

"Mine's Captain Madison. Jefferson Madison. You speak any Indian?"

"Mohawk," Peter said. "I know some Mohawk."

Captain Madison offered Peter his cigar. "This council you speak of, man. Where's it at?"

Peter took a puff. He remembered Tota's prophesy about people of all the four sacred colors gathering in peace at a Great Council hosted by the Iroquois. But could this be the reality of Grandfather's telling? So soon?

"Smooth Water Longhouse," Peter coughed. "It's about twenty miles from here---back in the bush near a river." He handed the cigar back.

A voice from inside the bus asked, "Do you know the way?"

"I'm not sure. I've never been there but I have instructions how to find it."

Captain Madison hooked his arm around Peter's shoulder and ushered him inside. "Looks like we're going to the same place, my man. Kindly direct my driver to the spot."

Peter counted four more soldiers standing in the aisle with a white, clenched fist insignia on their black arm bands. They sat down atop wooden crates containing rifles and hand grenades and took up positions at the windows. There were no passenger seats. Gasoline smells bit at his nostrils and he saw olive-colored fuel cans with white stars on them stacked inside.

Peter grabbed for a hand rail as the bus lurched forward. "How goes the war?" he asked.

"Are you kidding, man?" the driver laughed. "What rock you been livin' under?"

"I been at my Grandfather's for the past few months. He's been teaching me ancient things. . ."

"Don't you have no radio?"

"Nah. All our batteries burned out a long time ago. Grandfather was a real traditionalist. He never had any electricity."

"Right," the driver laughed. "Ain't nobody got no 'lectricity--- that was the first thing to go." The driver glanced at Peter and his smile dimmed. "You're serious ain't ya man. You really don't know what's happenin' do you?"

Peter shook his head. "The only thing I know is that fighting broke out shortly after I left New York to be Grandpa's apprentice."

"You know anything about voodoo?" Captain Madison asked. "What's in the pouch?"

"Tobacco."

"Lemme see." Captain Madison opened the flap, plunged his hand inside and held a pinch of tobacco to his nose. "I guess you're right," he said smelling the tobacco and grimacing. "Phew. Ain't nothin' but Indian tobacco inside this thing." He put the flap down and put his hand on Peter's shoulder. "Sorry to be so rude but these days you can't trust nobody."

Winding along the gravelled road, the bus swayed like a subway train. Peter peered through two bullet holes in the windshield hoping he would recognize the trail marker Tota had explained to him. He worried that they might have missed it.

Pine trees covered the hills and beads of sweat dropped from the driver's forehead with each double-clutching and manipulation of the gear shift lever. Old, gasoline powered vehicles were valued because their mechanicals were repairable; parts were interchangeable. Solar vehicles contained micro circuitry and factories making electronic parts had been knocked out early in the war. Thus, the White skins had become trapped in their own technology.

"Are you some kinda medicine man?" asked Captain Madison.

"No." Peter shook his head. "Why do you ask?"

"Because the tobacco in your pouch contains some kinda spiritual message, doesn't it?"

"I'm not sure. It was my Grandfather's last request that I deliver it to the council."

"There'll be medicine men at the council, right man?" the driver asked.

"I don't know. But there'll be lots of elders there."

"How much further 'til we get to this here council anyway?"

Engine roar enhanced Peter's doubts as the bus gained speed to climb a steep hill. Perhaps they think I'm bluffing, he thought. But what are *they* doing here? They know every nation in the Iroquois Confederacy has declared it is obeying the Great Law of Peace and *cannot* fight in this war.

"How did you find out about the Grand Council?" Peter asked Captain Madison.

After a long moment, a smile pushed out the Captain's cheeks. "You just told us back there, man," he said softly. "But don't worry none, our mission is one of explanation."

"Explanation?"

"Right."

"Tell him Captain," the bus driver said. "You tell it best."

Captain Madison reached into a breast pocket and retrieved a package of chewing gum. "First off I got to preface what I say." He held out a stick to Peter.

Peter put the gum in his mouth. "Thanks," he said.

"You understand that all we are is AdArCom, you know, Advance Area Communications. . ."

". . .meaning it ain't up to us to do nothin' but supply communications to our CO" the bus driver added.

Captain Madison threw the gum wrapper at the driver. "Man, am I tellin' this or are you?"

"All right, all right."

Captain Madison began. "You see we don't usually get this close to the action but on account of enemy radio intercepts we were sent up here to check them out. Nobody, including yours truly, believed them."

"We came motorin' through the Alleghany Mountains," the driver said. He quickly put his hand over his mouth.

Captain Madison continued: "It was very hot so we stopped beside a river to fill our canteens. Strangely, the usual water pollutants were non existent and I immediately became suspicious. Upstream, the men found several fish floating along with their bellies turned up. Usually dead fish are stiff but these carcasses were pliable as rubber. It was like they'd just been cooked. Man, we didn't touch that water even though our tests checked out A-OK."

"Tell him about the bugs, Captain."

Peter snapped his chewing gum. "Bugs?"

Captain Madison nodded. "We entered a strange wooded area 'bout a mile from the stream. All the trees were bare yet there wasn't a single leaf on the ground. . ."

"There wasn't any grass either," said the bus driver.

". . .it looked like the whole area was contaminated. We broke off several branches to check out the trees and found out that they were still alive. Some of my intelligence reports said that the enemy had suffered attacks from insects so I decided to make camp. I was sure the place had been disinfected 'cause of the sulphur smell that hung in the air."

"Man, the whole woods smelled like a hospital."

"We were taking specimens of soil for laboratory analysis when suddenly the ground burst alive with thousands of beetles! They just seemed to squeeze up from nowhere. I thought we'd disturbed a hibernation of some kind. . ."

"Man, we ran back to the bus and got the hell out of there fast as we could," the bus driver said. "You probably think we're crazy, huh? But it's the truth sure as I'm sittin' here drivin' this bus."

"Have you ever heard of anything like this happening around here?" Captain Madison asked.

"I haven't," Peter said. "But the elders and people at the council are very knowledgeable about such things. I'm sure they'll be able to help you find the explanation you're looking for."

Reaching the end of its long climb, the bus lugged onward bouncing in rhythm with the whine of its low gear. Peter noticed a stand of white pine trees, their tips all pointing skyward like cathedral spires. In front of them, a single white birch with a broken trunk lay pointing toward a break in the woods.

"Turn here," Peter slapped the driver's shoulder. "Follow those tire tracks through the woods, there."

For five miles the bus twisted and groaned through the bush.

Twice the men got out while the driver rampaged it down steep embankments. When the men filled their canteens with clear, cold water, deer tracks were sighted in the stream bed. Silver flashes beneath the water gave evidence of fish and beaver slaps sent partridge whirring from cover. A crow seemed to laugh at them and a speckled woodpecker tapped out a message as if in a private code.

They went over a rise and entered a lush valley. Peter saw a huge swamp elm tree that put everything else out of perspective. It dwarfed a big longhouse made from elm bark and made several old pickups, cars and travel trailers look like toys. Camping tents of different sizes and colors interrupted the green landscape. Two tipis, decorated with Northern Cheyenne and Dakota designs were being erected but Tota told Peter many more would be rising on this day. This gathering would host thousands of on-kwehon:we who knew the interpretations of their prophesies.

As they drove up and parked, a white man with flowing red hair sat atop a rock and appeared to be meditating. The driver pulled out his pistol and took careful aim.

Peter tapped him on the shoulder. "This is a sacred area," he said. "There can be no killing here. If that man is here, he is a good man."

"Oh, man," the driver grimaced. "The only good white man is a dead white man."

"Guns aren't allowed here," said Peter. "You guys should all leave your weapons in the bus."

Council had begun and when they went inside the dark longhouse, whispers and shadows accompanied their strides across the dirt floor. A pungent smell of smoke bit their nostrils and layers of it hung in the air to burn unaccustomed eyes. There were no windows, the only light came from squared smoke holes in the roof.

A crackling orange fire cast an eerie glow on the solemn faces of the rotinonhshon:ni chiefs. As Peter's eyes adjusted, he could see women in buckskin dresses coming into view from an opposite door. They all had pleasant smiles and their eyes sparkled through the dim light. They sat together and most appeared to be very old.

As the six soldiers sat down, Peter recognized the three upright eagle feathers of the Mohawk kasto:wa. He told the men to stay seated while he went to talk with one of his chiefs. The Rotiyane:shon all sat on benches. Wampum belts lay in front of the Onondagas, their purple colored beads contrasting with white ones to remind everybody of the ancient messages they held.

The Mohawk chief stood and spoke in his language to the 'younger brothers' who sat across the fire. After the interpreter finished, Cayugas and Oneidas all nodded in agreement. A Cayuga chief rose and addressed the 'older brothers' in his native language and after the interpreter finished, Mohawks and Senecas nodded.

"It's okay for you to talk in the English man's tongue," the interpreter said slowly. "We don't wish to offend any of our guests. But I caution you to beware. I might need help with some of the foreign words."

Peter stepped forward and the room fell into silence. "I've come here to deliver this pouch for my Tota. It was his last wish that I deliver it to you. It contains tobacco." He took off the pouch, held it up and put it beside the wampum belts.

An Onondaga chief, his face expressionless and lined with furrows of age asked: "Who are those that are with you?"

"They seek your counsel regarding a mystery they witnessed. They asked me for the answer but I'm unable to help them."

Captain Madison stepped forward and removed his beret. "I'm Captain Jefferson Madison, AdArCom, third regiment," he cleared his throat. "I'm pleased to be addressing such a distinguished body of leaders. . ." After finishing his story, the room became filled with nodding heads and murmurs. "Do any of you know what caused the bugs to attack us?" He took off his sunglasses. "We'd appreciate it if somebody could advise us how to prevent this from happening again."

An old Roya:ner stood up. His beaded rosette carried a wolf design and it bounced against his moose hide vest when he straightened. "I know of what you speak," his voice crackled. "The Peacemaker said the battle which now rages would become so violent that the mountains would waver. The rivers would boil causing fish to turn over on their bellies. There would be no leaves on the trees in those areas, no grass, and beetles would squeeze up from the ground to attack the combatants." The old man smiled. "Now you tell us you have seen these very things with your own eyes?"

Captain Madison nodded his head. "All the men seen it," he said.

"I cannot tell you how to prevent this phenomenon from recurring," the elder continued. "I can only tell you that it will happen until the fighting is ended. Go back to your people and tell them what you have learned. Let it be known that they are welcome to sit beneath our tree of peace as brothers just as the white man is welcome. Do not be disgraced if none come with you. Your path can only be decided by Sonkwaiatis:on and there is little you can do to alter it.

"Take as many provisions as you need for your return journey as we have plenty, but do not kill any two legged, four legged or feathered being while you are among us."

When the old man sat down, men's guttural voices and women's higher tones created excited crescendos of Iroquois sounds. Shrill war whoops split the air and one of the clan mothers began a chant which everybody picked up. Peter began talking with an elder and didn't notice Captain Madison and his men leave the longhouse.

After completing his conversation, Peter found the Soul
Brothers busily loading provisions aboard the school bus. Women
had brought bark plates heaped with venison and wooden bowls
teeming with corn soup. They had eaten and were filling gas cans
with water. Peter stepped inside to talk to Captain Madison.

"Hey, here's my man," the Captain said. He pushed a stick of
gum toward Peter. "Take one," he gestured.

Peter put it in his pocket. "I'll save it for later," he said. "You
guys leaving tonight?"

"Right now. My driver says he can make it back to the highway
before dark and we're already two days behind schedule. My CO
gets cross as a goose when you're late; gets real mean if he thinks
he's been had. I don't believe he's going to buy our story---ain't
scientific enough for him---but hell, it's the truth. A man just can't
do no better than that."

"Tell him he's welcome to come here for verification if he
doesn't believe you."

Captain Madison looked over the top of his sunglasses and
smiled. "Well, it's like this, Peter," he said. "Me and the CO got
sort of an exchange plan going with chicks, you dig? An' it so
happens I've got one that he just can't do without, you follow? So
don't worry, he'll be cool and chill out." He happily cracked his
gum. "What about you? You riding back with us?"

"No. They're going to burn Tota's tobacco tomorrow morning
at sunrise ceremony. I need a lot of spiritual guidance during this
period of my reawakening. Will you find your way out okay?"

"No trouble baby. I always find my way back from where I
been."

Peter shook hands with the men and hopped outside. He stood
beside two kids who wore baggy T-shirts and shorts. They heard
the engine start, gears grind and watched the old school bus until
it disappeared among the pine trees.

He wondered if they had understood the old chief's message

and doubted that any of them would return. Their destiny was charted by a power they knew nothing about. They were African foreigners just as the white men were European foreigners and neither had learned to live on Turtle Island properly. Tota told him neither would survive just as the black and white serpents didn't survive in the prophesy.

It occurred to him *their* message, not Tota's tobacco, was the real reason for his pilgrimage to this camp. After counselling with his chief, he felt honored to be selected to perform a role in the destiny of his people. Tota told him that Sonkwaitis:on hadn't turned his back on the rotinonhshon:ni. Instead, the past six hundred years had been a test to humble them and test their survival skills. It was still an onkwehon:we job to take care of Mother earth and soon they would be again be practicing the greatest of all duties.

Peter felt peace within himself and realized he could attain fulfillment. He'd enter the pine forest just like his ancestors and learn to weave himself back into the texture of Mother Earth. When his mind was pure again, and in harmony with the web of life, he'd wait inside the Longhouse with his people for the light that would come from the east.

Flight

I must look like one of those car commercials; the ones where a high-performance zoomer sweeps through a batch of leaves causing miniature tornadoes. Except that it's the January thaw, the roadway's a steaming, black ribbon with a dusting of snow on its shoulders, and the little tornadoes glisten. Now that I'm off the Reserve, I'll have to slow down.

I'm too old to be driving like a teenager, but the top's off my three-year-old Corvette and the wind, humming past my ears, is infectious. As out of place in this farm belt as a tractor in Times Square, an old Lockheed jet fighter sits up on the hill. I heel and toe my way down through the gears, swerve beneath it, trounce the gas pedal and listen to engine roar overcome tire squeal. Tutela Heights Road is narrower, has more bends and will be more fun.

Straight ahead, through veins of what in summer are hedges, stands a granite, library-looking building with white columns. I know this mansion and it seems to be beckoning. I slow down, turn onto the red, patio-brick driveway and stop between gateway posts.

Everything seems to be the same except smaller; the driveway used to be red cinders. I look to the right of the thick, arched doorway and expect to see Mandi peek out. Ah, Mandi. Her face beams up in front of me as I twist off the key.

She had the confident, bouncy stride of a fashion model and used it from the doorway to the teacher's oversized desk. Her skin, white as a trillium, made her blue eyes seem larger than they were and when she turned toward class and smiled, a magical quality beamed. Everybody fell silent while she patiently waited for Miss Ormsby to acknowledge her presence.

In those days, after a bouncy, morning school bus ride from the Reserve, I woke up to Bill Shostrum's latest tale of misadventure. Painfully shy, I was poorly dressed and hadn't yet realized my Mohawk point of view. Interrupted in mid-sentence by the girl's smile, Bill's face pushed into a predator's grin but to me, always on the brink of some masterwork, my painter's eye held a different value.

Slouched behind a row of leaning books, Miss Ormsby peered above her bifocals and pointed at me. "You'll have to sit in front of Jim Silverheels, there." The girl's smile changed to a look of purged innocence I knew must be captured on canvas. I had applied for that assignment the moment she passed through the doorway.

Amid a concert of mutterings and chucklings, the girl suddenly announced: "Hi! I'm Mandi Tannerhill and I've just transferred from Balboa High School, San Francisco. I'd really like to meet each of you and get groovin' here as soon as possible. I'm an up person and I've already missed out on a half year of activities." The buzzer sounded and everybody scurried to class.

Her magical aura drenched us all and those who would pursue her wasted little time. But the only one who seemed to interest her was a university senior---Harold Teaman III. Everybody knew Teaman divided his time between permissive girls, cars and Molson, but nobody knew his preference. Though impolite, reckless and crude, his droopy eyes and sea gull lips drove the girls wild. He spent money as if he printed it himself and could afford mediocre grades since he would someday inherit his father's realty fortune. He found Mandi and romance blossomed and I continued to discreetly admire the back of her blonde head.

In March, I began painting election posters for Randy Nymeyer, a hockey friend who had manipulated me to make and distribute them. Two months later he won by a slim margin and with a politician's grin invited me to Mandi's house for a victory celebration. With only two weeks remaining before finals, asking Mandi to model for me could no longer be avoided.

On the eve of the party, rasping along Tutela Heights Road on my celery-coloured Vespa, it struck me that I'd never partied off the Reserve before. As I approached Mandi's massive estate complete with columns, hedges and circular driveway, I suddenly realized that I lived a lot farther away than the six mile distance listed on maps. I bounced past my target to Lion's Park and sat beside a familiar friend, the Grand River. But after seeing Mandi's reflection in the water, I went back, leaned my motorbike against a hedge and like a beetle marching into a campfire, plunged inside.

Arriving in Indian Time gained me nothing but the butler's icy stare. His bald head and stiff, penguin-like manner sent a chill down my spine. "I, um, I'm Jim Silverheels and I've. . ." He raised an eyebrow, pointed a gloved hand toward a columned archway and sighed. My attention split between fascination and curiosity and I poked around the mansion seeking acquaintance. Grateful Dead music bawled from hidden loudspeakers as if in competition with the human ruckus from crowded rooms. Older girls, obviously Teaman's university friends, looked like halloween people; their waxen faces mirrored the Joker on the Batman TV show.

Somebody flipped a bottle of beer at me and it spilled on my shirt before I caught it. After wiping foam away, I stood behind three fraternity types and peered into a living room gathering. To the 4/4 beat of music, Meryl Steiner, an honour student, twitched her backside and heaved her breasts; arms flailing the air like a hovering bird. A partner stood snapping his fingers and clicking his heels in 2/4 as if somewhere else. I saw Mandi and waved to her but she pivoted and melted into the crowd.

I retreated down the hallway, found an abandoned leather chair in an empty room and slouched. I took a sip of beer, the sting of its taste making me grimace. Forcing three more swallows, the foam expanded, squeezed from my lips and went up my nose. At the same time, Bill thrust his head inside the doorway. "Here you are," he said. "You got rabies or something?"

I wiped my nose. "No, it's herpes."

"I knew you'd be here," he said. "You're alone, eh?"

"Yes I'm here and yes I'm alone," I said, happy to hear a familiar voice for the first time since arrival.

A devilish grin swept over his face. "It's okay," he whispered. Two motorcycle types emerged from behind him. "Close the door, Derek, we can turn on in here." He held a brown, smouldering wick and it struck me that they had some firecrackers.

"What have you got there?" I asked.

"Grass, Jim my boy, just some grass."

They sat on the floor Indian style passing a soiled cigarette with great reverence and soon the room filled with sour smoke. I watched Bill go from nervous giggles to uncontrolled laughter and finally he insisted that I take a drag. But I didn't want silliness, I now fantasized stealing off into the night with Mandi; perhaps the beer was taking effect. Nobody objected when I left the room and I concluded that gluttony is the only code among dopers.

Outside, blue lights slashed through the darkness washing faces in an eerie hue. A sniffling girl leaned on me to get back into her shoes; in this light her face took on the look of death. Sobbing, she ran off into a shadow and vanished like a special effect in a movie. I circled a poolside patio and saw Mandi. She was locked in Harold Teaman III's arm and they drank from each other's wine glass. I worried that soon she'd be adding his numeral to her name. I approached them but III gave her a lusty kiss and she returned it. I grabbed an ale bottle from a passing silver tray and chug-a-lugged half of it before a burp forced me to quit.

Couples were dancing and I caught Cindy Pete's stare. The only other Indian here, she stood alone between two shivering bathing suit groups. According to Bill, she liked me and I squeezed forward to test his claim. Suddenly, two muscular types, their bodies glistening from a coating of water, clutched Cindy under the armpits and solemnly carted her toward the pool. She kicked and punched at them, but her efforts were too delicate and they threw her into the water. They ferreted out another victim and it became plain that the girls considered dunking a badge of popularity. After heaving two more shrieking bodies into the water, they looked my way and I fled through double-glass doors.

I had entered a fancy gaming room and beyond a ping-pong table, a massive, green-felted Brunswick stood. Sipping my ale, I slid into a gallery chair and saw two guys trying to play Eightball. Eventually, they challenged me and it took only two rotations to send them searching for refreshment. Frustrated with my shyness, yet comfortable in these surroundings, I decided on a game of double cushion.

After dropping eight consecutive banked shots, I heard light applause. Mandi tapped her fingers against an opened palm; Harold Teaman III was at her side. At school, she always wore her hair up in a bundled concoction but now, it squeezed into a tail and flowed over a naked shoulder. Her pastel-striped purple dress looked like a nightie, its slit stopping midway up the ripple of her thigh.

"Wow," she breathed. "I'll bet you could win my father."

Attempting Bogart toughness I said, "Sometimes you get lucky." Though I ignored Teaman, I hoped he'd challenge me to a game.

In a backward glance, she said, "Babe. . .why don't you go back to the bar and get us a refill." Her eyes shifted back to me. "Or do you follow the code of Handsome Lake?"

"Ah, yes, sometimes. . ." Surprised at her mention of an Indian thing I wanted to pursue it further. But somehow abstainer Handsome Lake's goals didn't seem applicable in this setting. ". . .but this isn't one of those times."

Harold's face grimaced and he left the room sandwiching cuss words around something about white slavery while I lined up my next shot.

"I'm glad you're here tonight," Mandi began. "I've been *frazzled* to meet you."

I stroked the cue ball, being careful to conceal my pleasure at the way things were going. Bumping the required two cushions, it sent the six ball into a side pocket, kissed the eight into a corner pocket and stopped in front of Mandi.

"Oh-wow," she said. "Tell me true, do you feel that you play pool better than you paint or vice versa?" She picked up the ball and held it, arm cocked, as if she were going to take a bite from an apple.

"How do you know I paint?"

"Randy says you painted the election posters for him. I thought they were *totally* awesome."

"Oh, those things," I shrugged.

"Things?" her voice raised. "They were pos-o-tively top zoot. Did you paint all of them?"

"The ones with the faces. The other ones were done by others."

"The one that hung over the entrance to the munchroom really freaked me out. It had like, karma, ya know?"

"It's gone," I said, wondering what carma is.

"Yes," she sighed. "I asked Randy if I could have it but the day before the election, it disappeared." She put the ball on the table. "So now I guess I'll never have an o-riginal Silverheels." She slowly pushed the ball toward me with the heel of her hand.

"My important work is in oil," I said, leaning on my stick. "The water base and poster paper were practise in technique."

"Your technique then, ha-ha, is very good. After all electing a president is major shit. Those posters are cosmic---I'm not kidding, they really are."

"Would you like to see my oils?" I gushed.

"I'd be delighted."

"What about III?"

"Harold? Don't worry about him. He's been hitting on girls all night. He thinks that if he makes me jealous I'll go home with him in the new van he got for graduation." She smiled. "His father gave it to him before finals in case he doesn't graduate. Harold says he's going to break it in tonight with or without me." She glanced out the doorway. "Check it out," she looked at me and pumped her thumb twice in hitchhiker fashion. "His Oneness is dancing with Sarah Ryan right now. . .a Gemini and a Scorpio? Give me break. Meet me at the guest closet in 15 minutes!"

I worried that my Vespa would be inadequate in her eyes; I wished it would change into a Corvette. But when she saw it, she proclaimed, "your vrrroom is rrrad," hopped aboard and clasped her hands around my belly. "This is bitchin' she said, bouncing up and down. "Let's goooo. . ."

Her electricity tingled through me. With no driver's licence, no plate and no headlight, I couldn't afford a problem with the laws, so I aimed us down the shortest route and we buzzed into the balmy night at full throttle. When we hit the gravelled roads of the Rez, I slowed down savouring her closeness.

In the basement, I proudly displayed my work. After Mandi inspected it she seemed. . .settled. She studied a portrait of my sister using a manner that suggested previous art training; she had singled out my best effort. Still, I wondered about an inner thing that seemed to grip her.

"I like this one very much," she said, breaking her trance. "Your use of colour and warmth of execution suggest great involvement with your subject. Who is she?"

"She's Emma, my older sister."

"There's a lot of love in your work."

Astounded by this analysis, I felt naked. How did this stranger know about me? What had I revealed? Suddenly, I wanted to know all about *her* background and why rich people automatically know about art. Instead, afraid of more mind reading, I asked: "What time do you have to be home?"

"When the party's over."

"Well, it's all ready pretty late, eh?"

"Nonsense." She turned away from the portrait. "Daddykins has complete faith in my ability to handle any *pos*-sible situation."

I wondered what made her think I'd be interested in knowing that. "Well I still think you should. . ."

"You're afraid of your parents finding us down here alone--- aren't you?"

"Afraid? Of course I'm not afraid. They went to Turkey Point but even if they were---"

"Fishing!" Mandi's eyes widened. "That's what you do at Turkey Point, you fish, huh. When will they be back?"

"Probably tomorrow afternoon. But it depends. . ."

"Did you ever paint a nude?"

"Uh, no, not yet."

"Paint me then, naked. Right here and right now."

I felt my face flush. Who was this blonde witchy woman? Still, the total mysteriousness of her was exactly what I hoped to capture on canvas. I nodded.

Using a red velvet stage curtain rescued at destruction of an old movie theatre, I draped the heavy fabric into an arc on the basement floor. I formed folds and positioned a flood light beam so that shadows would lend a feeling of spaciousness. At first, I put a crystal vial containing a single yellow rose at the foot of Mandi's outstretched body but I removed it. Nothing should distract from her innocence. The mystery of her eyes would provide the contrast and perform the merger of directness with sensitivity.

My brush strokes took on an automatic flare, the colours came natural and before the sun came up, I knew I had it. My talent captured the exact interpretation I had perceived months ago. Then and only then did I allow Mandi her first look at my master-piece.

Standing behind me, in naked splendour, she stared at the dry-ing paint. "It's me," she whispered. "I guess it really *is* me."

"Of course it's you."

"I'm not a real person, am I?" she said, as if thinking aloud. "I mean I'm not a somebody, I'm a some*thing*. You know, a thing you couldn't love for real." Her eyes seemed troubled. "I guess I should thank you for capturing the *real* me."

I stood up to change my viewpoint fearing I had ghosted a skull or some other resemblance of black significance into it. "It's okay," was all I could say.

"Huh?"

"It's okay. I just checked it out and it's A-OK."

Suddenly, she wrapped her arms around my neck and kissed me. She hung on as if I were a cliff and I felt the wealth of her chest against my chest. Then she broke away, picked up her clothes and jiggled up the stairs emitting whimpering sounds. Was she crying or laughing? I thought about catching her and comforting her; things a friend would do. Instead, I signed the painting with my palette knife.

During the ride to her house, neither of us spoke. I had stolen her dignity, and guilt seeped into my nooks and crannies. Her portrait wasn't merely on canvas; she was notched on my easel forever.

"When are you going to bring me the painting?" she asked after hopping off in front of her house.

"When it's dry," was all I could say.

I didn't show the painting to anybody. It rested on its spattered easel awaiting the proper frame while I snapped a Polaroid shot for my portfolio. Paint and protective coating dried within two days but rain and strawberry picking forced additional delays. Finally, I tacked it into the most expensive gold frame I could find, wrapped it in grocery bag paper and carefully left the Rez for Tutela Heights.

When I arrived at Mandi's house, I parked behind a van in the circular driveway. Standing at attention in my best shirt, I clutched the portrait and whistled to the tune of the door chimes. At presentation, I planned to use the emotional high of the moment to advantage by asking Mandi to a lacrosse game. Suddenly the door opened and the butler tried to take delivery of my package. Finally, when he understood my mission, he promised to announce me and waddled down the long, marble hallway.

Mandi emerged from a doorway. "Oh." Her sandals slapped toward me. "You've got it." She took the portrait and when her snicker turned into a giggle, she covered her mouth. "Well, uh, thanks for the painting. Is there anything else you wanted?"

An icy chill exploded inside. "No, no, I guess not." My eyes sank to the marble floor and I heard shoes clacking.

"Ah," Harold Teaman III said, peeking over Mandi's shoulder. "You've brought the painting; good man, good man. Let's see it." He tore away the wrapping paper like a kid on Christmas morning, leaned it against a column and backed away to focal distance. "It's you, Man," he said. "The real you."

"Do you like it?"

"It's great, just great. He even included the vaccination mark on your thigh---nice touch Jim ol' boy, nice touch." He shook my hand, grabbed the painting and went out the door pulling Mandi along behind him. "Wonder what it'll look like in black light.

Too bad he didn't use those velvet colours; then your tits would have really stood out, eh? Ha-ha."

I watched the glossy van spray red cinders while it accelerated out the driveway. When it disappeared behind tall shrubbery, I heard the resounding echo of the door slamming shut behind me. I remember mounting the Vespa and sputtering home the long way, beside the river. It was early summer, but I was cold. Almost as cold as now. . .

I pull up the fur collar on my car coat, twist the key and the Corvette rumbles to life. I drive slowly toward the mansion, craning my neck for a look inside. Heat starts blasting against my trousers as I drive around the circle and go out the gateway. I accelerate briskly, take one last look, and hit second gear with precision.

A feeling of both relief and regret tugs at my tight lips, the relief finally cancelling the regret.

Resurrection

Silly Rubyann. From outside, she pressed her nose against the jewelry store's window glass for a better view of the object inside. This made her nose look like a pig's. Done by a 27-year-old reservation bred Mohawk Indian woman, this city child antic was unlikely. Rubyann pitched back, shaded her brown eyes from sunlight reflection and squinted. A turtle shell rattle bore the heat of her stare.

Anthony, her live-with man, didn't notice her focus until she tugged at his hand and fetched him. In the window's display, the rattle lay partially hidden under strings of sweet grass amongst flawless pottery with Mimbres designs and woven Chemehuevi baskets. Anthony guessed at what her favored Indian thing would be; perhaps it was the silver Zuni squash blossom necklace, turquoise watchband or rings. These are what he saw.

"I'm going inside," Rubyann said.

She released Anthony's hand, pulled at an oversized brass door handle and made an entry bell jingle. Anthony, realizing the shop was actually a jewelry store, joyfully followed. He applied authority to shut the stuck door behind him which triggered its etched window to rattle.

Rubyann went straight for the display. A brass rod held white, pleated draperies which provided a backdrop for the colorful Indian pieces. She leaned over the rail and eagerly reached for the turtle shell rattle. She uncovered its buckskin wrapped handle and in a swish held it up between them for Anthony to see.

"Are you supposed to touch that?" was his concerned message.

"This is it," Rubyann breathed. She began delicately fondling the lumpy, cantaloupe sized shell. "I'm sure this is it." She held it to her nose and sniffed.

Somewhere inside Anthony, where his Italian paranoia lived, a warning light went off. This was definitely another dot in Rubyann's recent behavior pattern. Ever since some fed up Mohawks, at a faraway place called Oka had resisted the Canadian Army, Rubyann's normal yuppy persuasions seemed distracted. Her fellow Onkwehon:we resolved to prevent an ancient forest of pine trees from being destroyed by golf course construction. They had dutifully defended their sacred forest with guns and put their lives on theline for trees.

"Smell this." Rubyann held up the belly side of the rattle. "Nothing smells like a turtle," she goaded. "You'll never forget it."

Anthony sniffed. "Just what is it that I'm supposed to smell?"

Rubyann pushed the rattle against his nose. "Now take a good smell," she demanded. "This shell's pretty old---you have to really get into it."

Anthony, now 40, wondered about his suddenly aggressive soul mate. In the decade they shared, he'd never seen her like this except when he had introduced her to alcohol at what he guessed to be her first cocktail party. She had foregone the after effects of sipping too much white wine and became violent. That night he got slapped. Though he had always suspected she was provoking something bigger, he never knew what.

"I don't smell anything," Anthony said. Believing he had made some sort of slip, he grasped the rattle, sniffed again, recoiled from an imagined sour odor and wrinkled his nose. "It is different," he uttered in monotone. He released the rattle to Rubyann before he realized that a third presence loomed.

"We have a policy here," came a frigid tone from an elderly man. "You break it and you have just purchased it." This thought seemed to actuate pleasure for a sweeping smile drove his steel-framed glasses up and his bald head rippled. "That particular item is valued at $350." He reached for the rattle palm outward.

Rubyann admired the lumpy shell at close range. It contrasted with the smooth veneer her brown skin gave to her high cheek-bones. "Buy it for me, Anthony," she said. "I left my purse in the car so I'll have to write you a check when we get back to the parking lot."

"Why do you want an old, smelly thing like that. . ."

Rubyann pulled him aside. "Because I helped my uncle, Oron:ia karon, make this rattle when I was a kid," she whispered. "It would mean lots to me if I could have it. . .sort of like a family momento."

Inside Anthony's head, blurry pictures spun like slot machine wheels. Family. So this has to do with family. Suddenly, three turtles stuttered to a stop like jackpot bars in a register window. Of course. That was it. Rubyann wanted the rattle because she is turtle clan. Didn't she reveal that piece of identity during one of their courtship discussions about North America being a turtle's back? He remembered something about Bears, Turtles and Wolves yet he couldn't be sure.

"I first saw it when I was four during a visit with Oron:ia karon at his log house on the Rez. I watched it hanging from a clothesline with wire around its neck. I remember how the blood dripped from its tail and formed a little pool; how it's delicate skeleton was attached to the shell."

"What's that? Looks like some sort of hole near where the tail should be."

"Oron:ia karon blamed it on somebody stupid. . ."

"Somebody stupid?"

"Somebody shot it with their .22 rifle. Luckily, it didn't hurt the turtle because the bullet hole's near the edge of the shell. That's how I know Oron:ia karon made this rattle."

"Wouldn't you rather have something of value? Perhaps a nice, Zuni ring you could use as a wedding ring?"

Rubyann's glare gave him his answer. It was the same scowl he had seen in a jewelry store the last time he had promoted discussion about weddings and rings. Still, Anthony schemed a plan to quench an unfulfilled desire. He'd buy an opulent, turquoise ring and see if an Indian thing would win approval for her wedding ring.

"You're an Indian, aren't you?" The old man flashed a smile at Rubyann. "You know, my great grandmother was flavored with some Indian blood in her. Cherokee, I think it was. What kind are you?"

"Strawberry," Rubyann said. She turned to Anthony as if expecting supportive retort.

Instead, Anthony pivoted and went to the window. This was an opportunity to quench his desire; he'd uncover Rubyann's preference. "How much is that ring in the window there? The bright blue one that's shaped like a turtle."

"You have excellent taste," said the shopkeeper. He reached for the rattle but Rubyann pulled it away. "That's Morenci turquoise." He breezed past Rubyann. "It comes from a mine out in Arizona. It's the only place where you can find genuine Morenci."

"Anthony?" Rubyann said. She hugged the rattle to her bosom. "I really don't want that ring or any ring."

"I have other rings if that one isn't suitable for madam," the shopkeeper said. "I've got an extra special ring I was saving for my daughter but I could let you have it. . ."

Rubyann asked: "How do you know that it'll fit?"

"Nooo problem. Any ring can easily be sized to fit any of madam's delicate fingers." He held up the ring between his thumb and forefinger so as to form a silver O. "You have beautiful hands, my dear." He presented the O to her so she could place her ring finger in it. "Do you play piano?"

"Was your craftsman an Indian?"

"Why yes, Zuni, I think."

"Try it on honey. . .go ahead."

"Notice the exact, miniature detail of the turtle. . ."

"I can put it on myself, thank-you," Rubyann said. She tucked the rattle under her arm, took the ring and slipped it upon her finger.

"It's gorgeous," Anthony said.

"A gorgeous ring for a gorgeous lady," the shopkeeper said.

Rubyann pushed her arm out and assessed the delicate turquoise ring. Its miniature turtle shell inlay and highly polished silver revealed superior quality. Normal Rubyann would have accepted this booty; she was fond of pretty things.

"How's the fit?" asked the shopkeeper.

"What's the price?" asked Anthony.

"It's nice, but I don't want it." Rubyann took off the ring and held it out toward the shopkeeper.

"But madam. This is an authentic piece fashioned by one of the foremost Zuni craftsman. Lucero, I think his name was. "

Rubyann flipped the ring in the air. It was Anthony who caught it. "What's the asking price," he said.

"I could easily sell this ring for $1,200. . .it's valued at much more than that."

Rubyann walked back toward the window. She began to rattle the shell in a slow, rhythmic beat. "Can your shiny ring cure cancer? This can."

"Bottom line," Anthony said. "What's your bottom line?"

"I suppose I could let you have it for, say, $1,000. It's so perfect for madam. I'd really like to see her have it."

Rubyann put the turtle shell rattle back in the window display. She held a sweet grass braid to her nose and inhaled deeply. She placed it atop the shell and arranged all of the braids into a camouflage clump. "Don't sell that rattle to anyone else," she said. "I'll be right back."

Anthony shrugged. "I guess she really wants that silly rattle," he said.

"Perhaps a diamond ring with a large stone would dissuade madam," the shopkeeper said.

Anthony sensed pending doom. He looked at the ring, gauged it's value and handed it back to the shopkeeper. "I guess she doesn't want it," he muttered.

"Let me get the other ring; the one I had specially made for my daughter. It's gold anodized silver and has coral, wampum and turquoise settings. I'm sure madam will find it quite attractive."

". . .and expensive, I'll bet. . ."

"One gets what one pays for. . ."

During his wait, Anthony browsed. Door bell tinkle followed by window rattle announced Rubyann's return. Anthony stood, with his hands in his pockets awaiting indication of Rubyann's mood.

She marched straight for the window, uncovered the turtle shell rattle and as she approached him, her eyes bristled with determination.

"He wants $350 but this one's only worth $100 to $125 tops."

She held up the rattle with authority. "The rule is: the smaller the costlier---because little turtles are harder to catch."

"Plus, this one's damaged," Anthony joined in.

"What's damaged?" A smiling shopkeeper held up a black velvet, ring box. "As I said, this was custom made to my personal specifications by a skilled, local craftsman. You'll note the wolf's head is in coral and set in wampum inside a turquoise-circle border."

Before Anthony could see, Rubyann thrust the rattle into his hands, took the ring and attempted to slide it on her middle finger. "How much do you want for this?" She struggled with a finger joint, slipped it off and pushed it on her index finger.

"I can't get it on," she said. "It's too small. . .do you have any soap?"

The shopkeeper pushed back his glasses. "Well," he sighed, "as I said, it can easily be re-sized. . ."

"Try it on your wedding finger," Anthony said. "If it fits, I'll buy it for you."

Instead, Rubyann slid it onto her baby finger. She quickly raised her hand to accommodate her audience and it slipped off and was propelled into the shopkeepers chest. Trapping it against his shirt, his head reflex sent his glasses askew.

"If madam pleases." He pinched the ring in an O formation with his fingers and straightened his glasses with the back of his hand. "I believe madam has one last wedding finger left." He slid the ring to her knuckle. "It fits," he said.

"It fits," Anthony said.

"It fits," Rubyann said.

They didn't agree as easily when it came time for price negotiations. The shopkeeper expected $1,000 for the rattle and ring but Rubyann would have none of it. Anthony challenged the jeweler to a gambling game he called Moola but to no avail.

Finally, since the rattle's shell was slightly damaged and his daughter didn't want the custom ring anymore because her dog had died and because he was part Cherokee afterall, the shopkeeper agreed to affordable terms.

As they left the shop neither spoke. Rubyann carried the turtle rattle next to her purse loops and every time a passerby gawked she'd hold it up and rattle the rattle. Anthony's mind computed several financial adjustment figures. They crossed the parking lot and headed, diagonally, for Anthony's sports coupe.

Before unlocking the car door he looked at Rubyann and meekly stood. Curiosity overcame him and pestered him until: "I know why you wanted the turtle shell rattle but why did you want the wolf's head ring?"

Rubyann seemed more radiant than usual. "Because it's my clan," she said, "wakkwaho: I am a member of the wolf clan."

Anthony almost snorted with surprise. He thought she was turtle family and that blunder had cost him. So is this about a woman thing. . .or an Indian thing? "Then the only reason you wanted the turtle shell rattle was for sentiment?"

"Sentiment and because we need it."

"What would we possibly need a rattle for?" Before *for* vibrated from his vocal chords, a possibility struck him like a thunderbolt. Maybe *they* wouldn't need the rattle but perhaps somebody else would. Like a baby. He fumbled with his door key and jabbed at the slot. "Are you. . .are *we* going to have a baby?"

He twisted the key and pulled the door open. A nervous smile fought with a sigh and he stared at Rubyann's face with anticipation.

"Of course not, silly," she giggled. "How could you be so silly? Besides being a keepsake, we need this rattle because it's a calendar."

They climbed inside the car and Rubyann told how the thirteen squares on the turtle's back were the moons of the year. She said that the outer ring usually has 28 separations for the days of each moon. This is what Oron:ia karon taught her while sanctifying the rattle.

Anthony twisted the ignition key and the engine rumbled to life. As Rubyann continued her story, pointed to each square and recited the name of its moon in the Mohawk language, Anthony admired the ring on her wedding finger.

The Last

Raven

Looking at Dan and Nola Goupil, you'd never guess they're
married. Not that they're unworthy but she's at least two heads
taller which makes you wonder how they make out physically.
They subtly administer the word of God each week, while we sit in
a circle trying to overcome hardness from the high-backed
wooden chairs. This circle is part of a continuing plot to get us
closer to God, nature, and each other by moulding us into a team
of young-adult Christians. Truth is, Sunday school attendance is
mandatory to play on the hockey team, which is why I'm here.

When I adjust my tie clasp, my elbow presses against the flesh of
a bare-armed fat girl sitting beside me. She brushes at the spot as
if removing bacteria, folds her arms with kindergarten precision
and places them in her lap. She knows I'm Mohawk and I know
that's why she brushed off her arm. Girls out number boys two-to-
one in this class and none of them drives you mad with desire.

"Well, Mr. Silverheels," Nola says, her voice one octave above a
whisper in true Christian fashion. "What do you think the meaning
of Christ's action toward the penitent woman at the home of Simon
the Pharisee was?" Hanging *Mr.* and *Miss* to surnames is supposed to elevate us to adult status, though we're expected to call

Dan and Nola by their given names. When the Goupils first arrived, I labeled this a get-acquainted trick, but I accept their ec-
centricities though its weird not being called Jim.

"What?" I say. "I...I don't think I heard the question. "I glance
toward Bill Shostrum and he flashes a devilish smile. He slouches
in his chair, the lapels of his blue suit flex into a diamond shape
exposing the too-short length of his polka-dotted tie. His punk
hair is greasy with hair goo and a glimmer from the ceiling lamp
reflects off his forehead. If you believe opposites attract, then you
know why we're chums.

Tracking the direction of my eyes, Nola says: "Now don't you
tell him the answer, Mr. Shostrum." The class laughs. She turns to
the fat girl beside me who's impatiently waving an arm.

"Yes Miss Breen."

Miss Breen leaps to her feet. "I think it's a story to remind us
that even though we're constantly submerged in sin," she says, confidence rampant in her tone, "Christ loves those who love." Satis-
fied with her brief moment of superiority, she directs a smirk toward me as she plops her oversized buttocks back into the chair.

"I disagree," I say. I'm not sure why this blurted out but now I'm
committed to explanation. I feel tension in the wily shifting of
everybody's eyes.

Dan Goupil glares at me and a nervous hush settles over the
room. He never enters class discussion but I can see he's interpreted my remark as an attack on his wife. He removes a hand-
kerchief, holds his plastic-rimmed glasses toward the ceiling light,
and huffs on the lenses. Wiping them with a fluid motion he says
quietly, "Exactly what do you disagree with, Mr. Silverheels?" A
smile curls his thin lips as he scans the class. "Surely you don't
challenge the love of Jesus, eh?"

"No sir," I say.

"Well I'm glad to hear that." The class translates his actions and
suddenly, I'm in a sea of snickering faces. "Well then, Mr.

Silverheels." He puts on his glasses. "*What* do you disagree with?"

"It's just that by forgiving this woman of all her sins, Christ is directing a lesson of humility toward Simon.

"Humility?"

"Yes. He's raised Mary Magdalen to a level of respectability above that of his host. He's used her to show Simon that her example of love makes her superior."

"You think Christ would *use* somebody for His own gain?"

"In this case, yes."

All eyes rest upon Dan. It's plain that emphasis has shifted from correct and incorrect and is now a question of vanity. To these people, Christ is their saviour; to me, he's a prophet. I realize Dan's next statement decides the outcome. He glances at his wristwatch and I'm reminded that it's almost time for dismissal. Perhaps I'll be saved by the bell.

Nola raises her eyes above an opened Bible. "Mr. Silverheels?" she asks. "What do you think Christ means when He says, "Therefore I tell you her sins, which are many, are forgiven for she loved much; but he who is forgiven little, loves little."

Dan brushes dandruff specs from his lapel. Simultaneously, shuffling feet and voices penetrate from the corridor outside. Looking at me, Dan says, "I think you've misconstrued the point of today's lesson. . ."

"Dan," Nola smiles. "I think you're *both* right." Everybody closes their Bible with a thump. "Now class," Nola continues. "Before all of you run off, don't forget our house-party this afternoon. We expect to have a lot of fun and I pray none of you will miss it."

I stand and file toward the door, a feeling of betrayal welling up inside me. If the objective of this class is participation, why haven't I been shown any mercy? Passing Dan at the doorway, I smile meekly. He squeezes my shoulder and says, "See you this afternoon." But I'm unable to answer.

On our way home, Bill and me and a skinny kid named Hart-

mann always stop at Gimpy's Diner. Our arrangement is we keep
Gimpy shovelled in winter and he lets us in on Sundays to play a
pin-ball machine everybody calls The Chief. Light up the 975,000
point feather and with Gimpy's verification, you get a dollar from
the Picnic Fund jar. In three years of play I've won twice.

"Are you going to the Goupils' this afternoon Jim?" Hartmann
stares at my reflection in the machine's glass panel.

"Not in a million years."

"What about you, Bill?"

Hartmann looks back at me: "What are you going to do?"

"I don't know," I say, tearing open my collection envelope.

"Hey!" Bill says. "Your parents are supposed to take mine to a
lacrosse game, eh? You're not going with them, are you?"

"No," I say. "The Warriors are in last place and they'll probably
lose again. I'll probably stay home and terrorize my sister."

"Get out of the way amateurs," Bill squeezes between Hartmann
and me. "Make way for the pro."

"Speaking of girls," Hartmann says. "Maybe I'll go to the
Goupils party. Linda'll probably be there."

"Nola's kid sister?"

"Yeah."

Inserting a quarter into the slot, Bill says, "Don't tell me you're
in love with Linda Switzer?" He jabs the coin return button with
the heel of his hand and takes out a jackknife. "Hey Gimpy," he
works the blade into the slot. "This damn thing's jammed again!"

"I wouldn't say I was in love with her," Hartmann says.

Gimpy walks over, scratches his belly, and pounds on the
machine. To Bill he says, "I don't know why you're the one who
always screws up this machine."

"Because he's just a big screw up," I say, overcome with clev-
erness.

"When they get older you gotta prime them a bit." Gimpy kicks
the machine and the coin clinks inside. Lights flash. Bells clang.

The caricature of an Indian in Sioux headdress swings his toma-
hawk and dances backward into starting position. "There. What
did I tell ya, eh?" Gimpy winks and limps back to his cleaning
chores.

"I wouldn't say I was in *love* with her," Hartmann repeats. "But
if you guys aren't going to be doing anything," he cracks a
knuckle, "then I'm going to the Goupils' party.

Bill launches his first ball. "Who says we're not going to be doing anything?" He pushes a flipper button as a wave of satisfaction
sweeps his face. "We're going to be shooting drunken crows this
afternoon."

According to Bill's latest plan, after our parents leave for the
lacrosse game, we're going to take our fathers' shotguns on a hunting trip. Bill says the radio reported that a flock of crows has been
gathering on the edge of town menacing people for several days.
Because of something called jurisdictional ingress and egress over
the woods they're in, nobody can do anything about removing
them.

"We're going to be big hero's, eh?" Bill says as we leave
Gimpy's. "We're going to do our duty and eliminate those haz-
ardous crows. Meet you at the bridge at two o'clock."

When my parents leave the house, my older sister curls up on
the sofa and flashes her beady eyes. "Sekhsa'tiyohake. Kanon
wahse?" she says in Mohawk.

She does this to aggravate me. We left the Reserve when I was
three and my family seldom speaks Mohawk here in Brantford.
Sometimes, when the house is full of relatives she gets everybody
going and there's always a point where they all look at me and
laugh. But she can't fool me. She wants me out of the house this
afternoon so she can cuddle with her boyfriend. She's hovering
around me like a fruit fly on a puckered apple and it's impossible
for me to get the shotgun from my parents' closet. To avoid suspic-
ion, I put on my new maroon windbreaker and depart for the

woods in street shoes.

I'm first to arrive. I sit on my favourite girder at the railroad bridge listening to creek water gurgle below. To the west a band of nimbus gathers on the horizon promising rain. Bill and Hartmann laugh while they goose-step the railroad ties, gleaming shotgun barrels propped between body and forearm. Bill wears a red plaid jacket and a ludicrous straw hat whose front brim is folded flat; BILL is inscribed there in red paint. Two ragged pheasant feathers jut from a hatband denoting hunting prowess. Hartmann's olive jacket has SMITH in stencil letters above his left breast pocket. They both notice I don't have a shotgun but say nothing.

I step atop a gleaming rail and gingerly keep their pace, my shoes making a tap-dancer sound. We hike down the straight tracks, grateful that railroads always take the shortest, most private routes. I've never seen more than two crows in the same place at one time and believe Bill's story to be false. We turn and cross a field, their heavy boots clearing a path for me through chest-high thistles.

We march toward a stand of hemlock when Bill signals to halt. From an opening beyond us, I hear a confused hum of shufflings and scattered caws. Perched amid saplings and clusters of lobe-leafed bushes, crows occupy the center of a u-shaped clearing. Bill and me are going to circle, leaving Hartmann stationed at the opening to block any escape attempts. To the northwest, the woods thicken, and, when we reach our position, the crows are between us and a barrier of trees.

Bill hands me a yellow box of shells and we begin. Each squawk, each shriek intensifies and it's plain we've been detected. It's so noisy I'm forced to cover an ear.

A sea of bobbing heads covers the ground like a rippling stadium tarpaulin. Branches bend in smooth arcs to accommodate squawking occupants. The crows compete for tiny red berries; they rape the bushes and peck each other in rages of greed. One bird leaps from a branch, frantically beats its wings, and flutters to the ground. These birds aren't drunk as Bill reported; most are too bloated to fly. Smaller crows retreat to the woods beyond but the majority continue their indulgence in spite of our presence.

Bill inserts two shells into his double-barrelled shotgun and closes it with a snap. Signalling Hartmann, he drops to one knee, cocks the hammer, and aims into a crowded sapling. I've been instructed to pass two shells into his palm and stand clear when spent casings are rejected. One hundred metres away, Hartmann slams the breech of his gun closed and raises its barrel in readiness. It's clear we've entered a world not intended for humans.

Bill's first blast shatters the air; my eardrums ring in response. Again he cocks, sights, and squeezes the trigger. *Boom!* He breaks the gun open and two casings spiral to the ground; a stench of sulphur bites my nostrils. "Shells!" he yells. I slap two cylinders into his opened palm like an intern assisting at surgery. An unexpected blast from Hartmann's direction makes me flinch. Bill smiles.

Fluttering and squawking, the crows are in chaos. Their numbers work against them; wings become entangled, foiling attempts to fly. Where Bill has fired into loaded branches, twin holes poke through the blackness. Leaning forward, he aims at the base of a crowded bush. *Boom!* His body jerks up with the recoil of the gun. In its panic, one crow hovers above us. It flaps its wings to escape but Bill blows it into an inkblot of swirling feathers. "Shells!" Bill shouts, waving away down-fluff. I barely hear him through the liquid hum in my ears.

Some of the crows fall to the ground; other scurry through the grass toward Hartmann. Some flap their wings, crane their necks and scold, but remain imprisoned in their branches. Hartmann concentrates his blasts on those who manage flight, his left arm pumping with mechanical precision. Bill can hit three crows with one barrage. It's evident from his cursing that he considers it a miss when only one falls. Hartmann lowers his weapon at the black army advancing toward him. His first explosion pours through their ranks like a splash of soapy water on a ship-deck, lifting and transporting those in its wake.

Drops of rain hiss against Bill's hot gun barrel but he continues his shooting oblivious of weather conditions. "Shells," he yells, blowing at smoke billowing from the breech.

A thunderclap booms across the terrain. The police must be on their way. "It's starting to rain," I shout, relieved at the possibility of leaving.

"Good," Bill says. "It'll muffle our shots." I hear the clink of shell casings dropping into a pile at my feet. "Come on, we've got to chase them toward Hartmann!" We advance, Bill firing every three strides. It's like walking through a plowed field, clods of black bodies occasionally squishing under our feet, the sensation plastic and awkward.

A crow deliriously wanders about the ground, dragging a broken wing. I stoop, hypnotized by its misery. It trips and falls forward on its side desperately clawing at the earth for traction. I reach to help, but it pops its smooth head between twisted wing feathers into a contorted position of defence. Eyes shrivelling with betrayal, it arches its neck to peck my hand. Instead, its eyelids squeeze shut, muscles relax, and it rolls over on its back. An eyelid pops open and an empty black sphere gazes at me. I scoop up cartridges from the shell box. I drop them into my pocket and tear the cardboard into a sheet. Covering the crow's body, I marvel at its design, reminded that things intended for a simpler function can be separated so easily from it.

When we rendezvous with Hartmann, a squadron of crows approaches head-on as if in attack formation. They are flying at eye level, their silhouettes barely visible against the backdrop of trees. In his haste to reload, Bill grabs a jammed shell casing and burns his fingertips. "Damn it," he winces. "Quick, Jim, gimme two more shells!" He loads, waits for Hartmann and takes aim.

Their first volley flashes with the ferocity of a howitzer; two crows erased in the blink of an eye. Bill's second shot hits its target too, but the bird's inertia carries it into his chest. Bill pushes it to the ground and squashes it with his boot. Hartmann's second burst is true, and the largest crow, bomber sized in comparison to the others, dives to the ground. Watching the crows falling like black snow flakes, I'm amazed at Bill's and Hartmann's skill at killing. Two crows peel off in an escape maneuver but Hartmann's capable pump gun sweeps them to obscurity.

"We got 'em Hartmann! We got every one of them!" Bill pushes his hat back. "Did you see how beautiful that big one rolled off and dove into the ground? Just like a Snowbird."

"Guess what, Bill?" Hartmann inspects his remaining ammo. "I hit that big one with my deer slug. You remember that deer slug I showed you?"

Bill nods. He blows at blue smoke rising from his barrels. "Hey, Jim" He slides a shell into the left chamber. "I want you to hit that crow in the tree over there." He closes the gun with a snap of authority and offers it to me.

I had hoped that Bill, consumed in his frenzy, would forget about my participation. Yet, like a substitute player sitting on the bench, I've been rehearsing all afternoon. "I'm not a very good shot," I say, not really wanting to be heard.

"Take it," Bill thrusts the weapon into my hands. "And don't miss."

I plant my feet, pull back the hammer and raise the barrel. Rain drops poke at the shoulders of my jacket; one ricochets off the stock and splashes into my eye. I squeeze my eyelid, accept the brief sting, and shake my head. Bill sighs impatiently. Raising the front sight into the crotch of the v, I fix it on the silhouette beyond. My target twists its neck in puppet fashion against the pink colouring of the uncertain sky. I hunch my shoulder, tighten my grip, close my eyes, and pull the trigger. *Boom!*

"You missed!" Bills grabs the gun, breaks it open, blows at the chamber and inserts one shell. "You don't sight a shotgun, stupid. You aim it with both eyes open. And don't pull the trigger, *squeeze* it!" Bill hands me the gun. "Don't miss this time---this is the last one."

I wipe my brow, seat the gunbutt against my shoulder and pull the hammer back. I take a deep breath, raise the barrels, and sight according to Bill's advice. Suddenly, the crow kicks away, flaps its wings and climbs toward the horizon. I follow it and calculate its path. Hatred in the dying crow's eyes nags my mind but it's erased by my passion for success. Squeezing the trigger, I can almost see the pellet pattern sink into the feathers. "I got him," I say, exhaling. Wings spread like sagging semaphores, the crow glides breast first, bouncing in slow motion as it hits the ground. I feel a surge of triumph. I try to push my face into a smile.

Bill slaps my shoulder. "Nice shooting," he says, taking the gun.

Sheets of rain force us into the woods seeking shelter, but sunbeams isolate the clouds and begin melting them. Each imprisoned with our own thoughts, we view black specks dotting the landscape. Blotches of blood coating tree branches, bushes and grass begin washing away. Divots in the ground smooth their sores but severed branches remain permanent scars to today's memory.

When sunlight finally blasts through, we cross the peninsula toward the tracks, the ground sucking at our feet. Bill ransacks the largest black feathers and adds them to his hatband, his singed fingers provoking an occasional grimace. In a show of humanity, Hartmann plods across the field, finishing off dying survivors with his gunbutt. I pick up a shell casing and blow on its open end, the lonely whistle recalling the dead crow's eye and its echo of emptiness.

Beneath the bridge, I wash mud from my shoes with a gnarled

twig. I notice a brown spatter of blood on my pant leg. It's partially dry and I splash cold creek water on it to prevent a stain. Gusts of wind, already frigid, push at bushes along the bank sending messages of winter to those who are listening. I gaze at Bill and his Medusa-like headdress. A feeling of sardonic ridicule blossoms inside me, but humility pacifies the notion.

The Private Strangers

They always met trusting fate to either grant or overlook rendezvous and neither broke this one rule. She would arrive in San
Jose Monday afternoon from a Los Angeles commute flight and
shuttle to the Casa Alvarez Hotel. This is where she stayed for three
days every month and where Simon sat on a bar stool listening to
piano tunes in the lounge. Both were in a position to adjust their
sales trips to coincide but scheduling their tete-a-tete was considered a no-no. That would take the buzz of chance out of it.

Before meeting Joyce, Simon drove a company car down the
peninsula from San Francisco and returned home each evening.
Increased sales orders, freeway traffic and his wife's growing re-
pulsion gave him excuses to take advantage of a nonrigid lifestyle
and lucrative expense account. He always drove Joyce to the
nearby airport when their time together expired---they always sat
in quiet gloom like paratroopers awaiting jump orders. Then is
when he'd tell her.

Talk of family, friends or job was another taboo but with a five
year history together they could afford elimination of personal
topics. Among the few basics that Joyce collected was that Simon
was a Mohawk, married with a teen-aged son. Simon knew Joyce

to be twice divorced with no children. These bald facts were never expanded upon and never discussed. Their world was them and they revelled in it.

"Hi," she whispered, placing purse and gloves atop the bar. Her thin face was cold and white as soapstone, it took on full dimension only when she smiled.

He quickly ordered two dry martinis and slid out a bar stool. "You look abso-*rutely* marvelous," he said mimicking comedian Billy Crystal. "Abso*rutely mah* velous!"

"You look absolutely divine."

This completed their salutation ritual but Simon sensed something wrong in the tone of her voice. It didn't have the usual girlish ring to it, perhaps she had a cold. "Do you feel all right?" he asked and she answered, "Yes but I've had a stressful day topped off by a bouncy flight." She pushed the martini away. "I really don't want this---I'm famished not thirsty." She smiled. "Can we go to the room." Simon picked up her luggage and carried it across the concourse to 77, the room Joyce preferred.

Simon enjoyed watching her prepare for dinner; was amazed at the feminine prescription that went into her illusion. He had witnessed her preparations before but on this occasion she seemed to project a different aura. He considered her a very handsome woman; one of a fortunate few whose bouquet beautifies with maturity.

Coils of long, platinum blonde hair surrounded her neck like telephone cord and dangled to her abundant breasts. Her complexion shone with a mother's purity and contrasted with the sultry, cosmetic tint of her large green eyelids. In summer, he noted that her lithe body magically turned Indian bronze though swimming always escaped their agenda.

He changed his shirt and necktie, appraised himself in the mirror and combed his wavy hair. He suspected his walnut colored skin and black hair were stuff that drove Joyce's interest in him; he believed opposites attract. Suddenly, he wanted to shout his message to her, but no, timing had to be perfect, he'd wait.

Slipping into a tweed sport coat he noted decorator changes to their room. Solids, stripes and danish modern had replaced floral, plaid and french provincial. A love seat where they first kissed was missing and an abstract nude hung suggestively above the bed.

"Did you notice the changes they've made to our room?" Simon cast a critical glance. "I wonder why they did it. It was fine the way it was." It struck Simon that the possibility of them being here together was infinite as the stars. Out of gratitude he stretched, kissed her temple and took in her woman smells.

"Things change," Joyce said. She stood up and twirled around. "I know we always go to Paolo's for pasta on Mondays but I'm in a Plateau 7 mood. Do you mind?"

"Of course not, my dear. I'm sure Julio won't have any trouble seating his preferred customers a day early."

During dinner, while awaiting his news opportunity, Simon remembered the first time they met. They had been drawn together as naturally as the sea to land, there had been no awkwardness about it. Rain threw a powwow they attended into chaos and they stood shivering, side by side, under a vendor's canopy flap. After waiting, waiting, waiting for it to clear, Simon offered Joyce a ride and she reciprocated with dinner at Plateau 7.

She taught him tennis and golf in summer, they watched movies and went bowling during the rainy season; recreation always followed by passion. Simon slowly relinquished powwow attendance which went unnoticed by his family since nobody went with him anyway. During monthly visits, they left their tryst-place between 8 and 10 a.m., and returned between 4:30 and 5 p.m. Simon knew he was at risk being with Joyce while she was in town but being discovered seemed irrelevant.

"There's a new Clint Eastwood downtown tonight," Simon

sighed. "Feel like taking it in?"

"Not really; I'm very tired." Joyce took a sip of wine. "I'd prefer to go back to the room and relax. We could watch TV or do some reading or something."

"I'd prefer the 'or something'," Simon smiled. He wondered why she preferred relaxation to recreation. She seemed burdened with thought but her burden couldn't possibly approach the one he shouldered; a dysfunctional marriage held together by an unsuspecting son. "Maybe you'd better consult a doctor, I'll make an appointment for you in the morning."

"That won't be necessary," Joyce said. "I saw my doctor three weeks ago. Don't worry, I'm fine; passed the physical in flying colors. To quote the doctor, I'm healthy as a horse."

"Sounds like you went to see a veterinarian," Simon laughed.

"Does it?"

He wanted a laugh here; wished she'd lighten up. He didn't want to begin on such a serious note. He'd attempted to break through her offbeat sense of humor before without success; it was his wife that labeled him a comedian and told him so regularly. For an instant he saw his wife, not Joyce, laughing her crude, hyena-laugh that always embarrassed him in front of his Indian friends. But that irritation would soon be over and his brain extinguished her quick as a new menu on a computer screen.

"You see," Joyce began, efficiently munching her salad. "I'm pregnant."

Simon put down his fork and wiped Roquefort smudges from his lips. "I don't know how they manage to have such crisp lettuce every time we come here," he said. "They must have a patch somewhere up on the roof."

Joyce laughed quietly. "I must say you're certainly super suave about this."

"I don't mean to be," Simon said. "And I certainly don't think it's funny, you're being pregnant. I think it's, uh, interesting.

"---a *crisp* situation, wouldn't you say?"

Simon replaced the napkin on his lap and watched her continue eating. He always assumed she used avoidance measures and now faced with fatherhood, regarded the final decision as hers---in his culture the women had say. He saw her condition as a surrender to her nurturing instinct; knew her biological clock was ticking. "What are you going to do about it?"

Joyce laughed aloud. "How typical," she said. "Good, old, *typical* Simon."

"I'm not typical and you know it. If you're pregnant it can only mean that you *want* to have a child."

"That's right, Simon, bull's-eye! I *do* want this child!"

Staring at her platinum hair, Simon's senses fogged with the bleak halls, white uniforms and scratchy doctor announcements of a hospital memory. Through antiseptic glass in the maternity ward, a nurse held up *his* son. It's too-large head appeared wrapped in floppy skin that didn't seem to be attached. And now that embryo had ballooned to full size, was only awaiting his, Simon's, signature on a dotted line to fly away in the talons of the Marine eagle. Never mind college. Never mind getting a degree to end up working at McDonald's. He said he could become a man by escaping his mother's grasp. With his son's flight, Simon too, would escape the clutches of a barbed woman. He asked: "You're sure you want this child?"

"Are you suggesting abortion?"

"No, of course not. How can you abort something from the Creator? It's just that it'll mean many changes---"

Joyce smiled. "It *sure* will," she said. "But let's not discuss this any further now. I really didn't mean to begin our visit with such personal news." She finished her glass of wine. "You're not mad, are you?"

"Don't be silly," Simon said. How could I possibly be mad at you?"

In room 77, picture beams from the TV tube had turned to blizzard patterns after the national anthem: one of Simon's insecurities, it was always on. A slosh of bathroom activity and the buzz of Simon's shaver irritated the air. Joyce lay sideways on the bed. Her platinum locks blended into the white satin sheets; a paperback book spread flat beside her. They always exchanged gifts on their first night, nothing fancy or personal, but her red peignoir and his golden colored tunic were examples. This time she contributed an initialed tie clasp; the D.H. Lawrence had been his gift.

During sex, Joyce surprised Simon; she seemed more vigorous than usual. Later, while huddled together savoring their ecstasy, it was he who broke the silence.

"I've got to tell you something important," he whispered.

Joyce sat up clutching the sheet to her bosom; her breasts had suddenly become private again. "No, *I've* got to tell *you* something," she said.

"*I think you should know,*" they began in unison.

Simon laughed. "Go ahead," he said.

"No, it's okay," Joyce said, in the lower octave range of her voice that meant serious.

"As a gentlemen, I insist---"

Twisting her hips to face him Joyce said, "The baby's not yours, Simon." She turned away. "You see, I'm getting married tomorrow and I came here earlier today to take care of transferring my orders to the home office---"

"*You're* getting married? Oh, get off it---you're putting me on!"

"What's the matter Simon, you think I'm incapable of marriage? That's always been your trouble, you've always considered me an ornament that came with the room."

"You're not *really* getting married. . ."

Her nod triggered something inside and he felt his bowels filling with hatred. "*I've* always considered *you* an ornament?" he said. "What about me? I'm the ornament here, the Indian flavor of the month that you picked up at a powwow, remember?"

"Let's be civil about this," Joyce said quietly. "I didn't have to tell you, I could've just disappeared, you know."

Attempting composure, Simon turned his eyes away. "Yes, I suppose you could have."

"He's really a wonderful person---we've been going together for about three months. . ."

Simon's eyes clouded with passing images and he barely heard her girlish tones. He heard only her laughter when she scored a strike; saw only the broad smile when she leaped the net in victory, the dainty way she held her knife and fork at dinner. He pictured *them* in the maternity ward, *he* holding her clenched hand, *he* comforting her through the fear of childbirth. Suddenly, he felt the fear of loneliness.

". . .don't you see. I mean after all, Simon, I'm a two-time loser that's never raised a family like you have and I don't want to miss out. I really love him. You and I are more like brother and sister with sex thrown in and I hope, I *know* we'll always remain the best of friends." Her face cast a diamond's shine; it's dazzle hard and cold.

"I hope you'll be very happy," Simon said. When he turned on his side he felt a hug and the bulges of her body squash against his back.

In summation, Joyce told him she was leaving on the 7 a.m. flight, her wedding was at two. Though invited, Simon declined. Headlight glows stuttered to oblivion through venetian blind slits and the whine of tractor trailer tires finally put Simon to sleep. Yet when the phone rang for wake-up call, he accepted the taped voice announcing time, weather-prediction and breakfast menu without remorse.

With a jurist's gaze, he evaluated a shapely leg peeking from beneath the sheet. Jiggling her shoulder, he noticed a half-lit face struggle to receive the morning, it was drab and ugly and Simon reeled in disbelief. She said she'd take the shuttle to the airport but Simon insisted on performing his duty.

They entered rush-hour's tangle with familiar precision; thoughts, words and deeds still bruised with sleep. In the terminal, the clack of Joyce's boots recorded their progress across the marble floor while her Pullman bobbed at Simon's grip in corresponding rhythms. At the boarding gate, he handed her the bag. She took it and kissed him on the cheek.

Joyce asked: "What's your news? You forgot to tell me." and Simon said, "My son. . .he's, uh, finally decided on college. . .and my wife and I are going to Massachusetts together to look over the campus."

"That's nice," Joyce said. "Goodbye Simon."

He watched her ascend the boarding ramp and vanish into the cave of the gleaming fuselage. He climbed the stairs to the observation balcony and leaned against an aluminum rail. He considered the probability of her return next month; she did say *transferred* not cancelled. Friendship was a good thing to have on your side, it could even outweigh love. She'll be back, he thought. Or will she?

In the distance, her jet approached take-off position and it occurred to him that he didn't know what her married name would be. Emitting a porpoise grin, the 727 turned in awkward splendor, revved its motors and began acceleration. As its parade of windows sped past, its nose raised and he almost shouted, "Come back. . .I'm getting a divorce. . .I love you," into the shrieking exhaust whistle.

A Jingle
For Silvy

My best friend, Silvia Longfish, says I'm just a backward Indian. She says she wonders why I never call her a forward Indian. Whoever heard of a forward Indian? She got that way when she moved to the city---she got fast. Silvy's been my best friend since we were babies and she's the best friend I'll ever have. I just wish we were still dancing together in powwows.

I wonder what Silvy'd do if she were here right now watching me beading my moccasins? She'd probably smell them; new deerskin's always so fresh and clean. I remember last year, when we were in grade five. She said she'd make the prettiest ones she could. Silvy's got this *thing* about pretty. Probably because she's so pretty herself. She said she'd enter them in the Ohsweken Fair. She said she'd probably win the red ribbon. Come to think about it, Silvy's got this thing about winning, too.

These moccasins are going to go real good with my new jingle dress. Like Silvy would say, I'm going to be colour coordinated. For the first time in my whole life everything's going to match. I'm trying hard not to go super-fast. I don't want to lose my quality beading rhythm. After a whole week's work, I'm almost finished. Good thing the Creator only gave us two feet.

Silvy gave me all her tiny seed beads when she left. They're the old fashioned kind with the weeny holes. I've already stuck my finger twice. Silvy probably knew that's what I'd do---she's smart like a fox.

Thinking about Silvy is making me impatient; I've used two beads that are the wrong shade of green. Great. Now I've got to rip out the whole leaf. Silvy never used to be impatient until she moved to the city. Her Mum got her a new Dad; he's even got blond hair. Now they got lots of money and a new motor home.

The day she told me, *she* was impatient. She said: "Well I'm going to the city now, I'm outta here, I'm going to be an *up*town Indian." Didn't matter a whole lot to me, though. It's not like I'd never see her again. I knew she'd be back. Even if it's only for the powwow. Maybe this time she'll stay. At least for the summer. Sooner or later everybody comes back to the rez.

"Hi Marcie," Delbert rushes in.

I don't know why people call us twins, on account of he's a boy. He's such a dweeb but he can make really-good jingles. He gets Tota's, Grandpa's, snuff lids and shapes them into cones. Normally, this takes a lot of skill and patience. But Delbert's not normal. Tota says he's a natural. He makes money selling jingles to other dancers. He even charges *me*. But I don't pay him any money. I'll just do his homework for the whole month of September or something. Good thing we're in the same grade. I mean school, not quality level.

"Here's your three new jingles," Delbert says. He's puffing like he just ran in the Tom Longboat marathon race or something. He drops them right into my bead bowl. "I couldn't fix the old ones. They were too flattened."

"Those old cones were real brass jingles. Gramma gave them to me. That's why I wanted them fixed, Dweeb."

"These sound just as good. . ."

"That's not the point. They're a different colour."

"So?"

"So you can't mix silver jingles with brass ones."

"Why not?

"They aren't colour coordinated."

"Well leave them off then," Delbert snorts. "You already got 250 jingles any ways. . ."

"Two hundred and twenty nine! I need 232 to make my outfit perfect."

"Tota says you're not s'posed to make things perfect. Only the Creator can make perfect things," he smirks. "That's why I leave a little space when I bend the tin."

"Tota doesn't dance in the powwow this afternoon. I do."

"You can just put all of them in the middle of the V. You know, where you got them ribbons coming into a V at the top. That way, everybody'll think you done it on purpose."

"Everybody but me."

I decide to make Delbert invisible. I didn't hear what he said on account of when you're invisible nobody can hear you. It works, so by the time I put three more beads on my leaf he's gone. I took his advice about putting the tin jingles on the top row in the centre. On account of Delbert's got expertise. I made the moccasins perfect, though. I figure now that my jingle dress is screwed up I'm still on the Creator's good side.

On the drive to the powwow, Mum gives me some gum to chew. I didn't want to chew it on account of my loose tooth. But I didn't want to hurt her feelings, either. When somebody gives you something you're not supposed to make them feel bad and not take it. Ever since Mum quit smoking she's always chewing something. Sure enough, out pops the tooth. I pick it out and put it in my jeans with my spending money. Then I put my tongue into the hole. Yecccch! It's all bleedy. I hate when this happens.

When we drive over the bridge next to the powwow grounds, I see the sun shimmering on the river. The water looks like a giant

jingle dress.   After we get to the parking lot, I figure its one
o'clock because the loudspeaker guy says, "Grand Entry in thirty
minutes. No Indian Time allowed." I don't know why we have to
always start on time. You'd think this was TV or something.

   Being skinny comes in handy at these kind of things. When you
have to put your powwow clothes on, it's lots easier to get dressed.
I know one of Delbert's tubby friends who has to start getting
ready a whole hour before Grand Entry. Trouble is after all this
work, I never know what I finally look like.

   Mum's talking to this white woman with a camera who's come
over to admire me. I hate when this happens. I also hate being
number 124. That extra digit makes my sign bigger which means
it'll cover up more jingles. Mum tugs at my number to straighten it.
As if it's going to stay that way. She's always tugging at something.
Sometimes she even makes my eyes water. Like when somebody
distracts her while she's doing my braids. Like now.

   "A:ki," I say fighting back the tears. "Ow! Ow! *Owwww*!"

   What can I do? You can't run away when somebody's got your
braids. All I can do is hope the woman isn't going to stay and take
my picture. I'll bet I've been photographed a zillion times. Silvy
gets her picture took lots. Even when she doesn't have her outfit
on. Nobody ever takes a picture of me when I'm just normal.

   Mum and that woman are talking about me like I'm invisible.
"She's really quite shy except in school and at powwows," Mum
says. "Yes, she likes to play ball with the boys, but no, she doesn't
have any boyfriends yet. . ."

   I'm so embarrassed I hope I *am* invisible. I'm beginning to feel
like an object when good ole Delbert runs up.

   "See? I told you," he says. "Those silver jingles look great." He
inspects one of his new jingles and then flicks my nose. "Gotcha.
Ha, ha."

   "Okay." Mum snaps her gum. "You're ready now."

   "Could I have a pict. . ."

"Ha, ha. Better hurry up, Dude." Delbert wisks me away with his hand: "They're all ready lining up."

Normally, I'd smack him but he just saved my life.

I shuffle off toward the assembly area. All of my jingles are gleaming and swishing. I sound just like rustling leaves in the fall. Silvy always meets me over by the garbage cans.

"Attention all dancers," the public address system cracks. "Would all dancer*squeeee*. . .please go to the assembly area. All dancers please go to the assembly area for Grand Entry. If you haven't registered yet they'll take you over there. Last call. All dancers to the assembly area."

I wriggle to settle everything. I hope none of Delbert's jingles fall off. I saw somebody's eagle feather fall off once. They had to stop the whole powwow and do this lost Feather Dance thing. On account of he's a Rotiskenrake:te, protector, I asked Tota all about it. I'd hate to have the whole powwow stop on account of me.

He said: "You can't insult a spirit. When a feather falls, it's the spirit of a fallen warrior. So four veterans, representing the four directions, sing two verses to the Creator and to the spirit of their fallen comrade.

"Then they sing four verses and charge the feather on the down beat of the drum. Those who have not taken coup will use an eagle fan because they are not strong enough to touch the spirit. After six verses, the honoured veteran picks up the feather in his left hand. He lets out a whoop to signify that the spirit of the feather has been captured."

Lucky for me all anybody has to do is hand back a jingle if it falls off.

"*Squeee*. . .Okay dancers. It's powwow time."

One of the Drums start up and its shrieking singer's begin their song. *Boom, boom, boom, boom, boom, boom-boom.* Six beaters mix their being in unison with the spirit in the hide. It creeps out to the dancers. I can *feel* it.

I'm really proud of these new moccasins. I can tell they're happy. They like to be at place where they're more welcome than shoes. I'm happy they will keep me connected to Mother Earth. I pray they will keep me on the good path.

In comes the Eagle staff bearers. Then some old guys wearing dark blue uniforms with medals on their chests. They carry the US and Canadian flags. They go clockwise to be in harmony with Mother Earth. Everybody is preparing to join the dance and enter the circle. There must be a zillion people here to watch. I adjust my number and look for Silvy.

I see her with the men's fancy dancers. She looks like a boy in her short, streaky haircut. She's also got on leather hot pants with lace edging and Luscious Red lipstick. It clashes with her dark complexion. It *must* be Silvy. I run up to her jingling away.

"Silvy?" I hope she doesn't get all emotional. "Is that you?"

Silvy casts a cold stare, the kind you see on statues. It's like her eyes are dead or something. She looks at my jingles and her eyes begin to soften. Here comes the real Silvy. I back off in case she's going to hug me. No sense getting all your jingles crushed.

"So." She cracks her chewing gum. "How you been 1-2-4?"

Silvy says she *loves* it in the city. Silvy says her mother's new boyfriend's got lots of money. Silvy says he takes her out to dinner in places with candles on the tables and stuff. Silvy says he's got yellow hair all over, then she giggles. I wonder how she knows this.

I'm consumed by curiosity, just like a cat. So when Silvy squeezes through the crowd and goes over to the river, I follow her. The powwow can wait. I wonder if she wants to borrow my stirrups?

So, you got any boyfriends?" Silvy picks up a stone and throws it into the river. "I got about five."

I look for a log to sit on. "Do you really have five boyfriends?" I fluff my dress and sit down.

"Yeah." Silvy giggles. "They all like my brown skin."

"Wow!" I think about having five Delbert's running around. "How do you keep track of them all?"

"It's hard. Sometimes I get them mixed up. Sometimes I call them by the wrong name. But they don't seem to mind. Like the time when I was having sex with Johnny." She covers her mouth and giggles. "I called him *Joey*!"

"*You* were having sex?"

"Well of course---don't you? Or are all you Rez Indians too backward around here?"

There she goes again talking as if she wasn't from here. She was born here and went to school here and lived here all her life. She knows everything I know about our tradition because on-kwehonwetsheraka:ion, old time Indians, taught us. She knows when you marry outside you're outside the sacred circle. She knows you shouldn't die outside the circle either.

"I thought about it once," I say. "Me and Kevin Sky got into some really radical kissing. Then things turned icky. He wouldn't take the gum out of his mouth."

Silvy looks at me as if she's disgusted. Her eyes go all cold again. Then she looks at her reflection in the river. I give her one of my stones to throw. Instead of seeing how far she can throw it, she fires it right at herself: *ka-splash* !

A boat full of people comes skimming down the river. Their motor sounds like a giant mosquito. When they see the tipis and all the people, their motor changes its pitch. Silvy comes out of her trance and looks at me.

She's my best friend but oh-heck-enit I've just got to know. "Do you like it?" I don't know why, but I look down and giggle.

"Doing it?"

Suddenly, I'm very uncomfortable. I'm not sure I really want to hear her answer. I wish I'd never asked. Silvy must be looking at me; I feel my face flush. She's close enough, maybe she'll smack me or something. I decide to change the subject but I can't figure out anything to say. It's like when you're in a bad dream and you try to holler for help and nothing comes out.

I sense something happening. I look up but Silvy isn't even looking at me. I must be invisible again. She's looking over my shoulder and I hear footsteps coming. I stand up.

"Oh shit," Silvy says. Suddenly, she reaches over and starts fondling my jingles. "These are really nice. How many of them do you have on your dress?"

"About 232," I say. I turn and here comes this dreamy blond guy. He looks like somebody from a men's clothing ad. He's walking right at us.

"Oh, here you are, Silvia," he says. "Who's your cute little friend?"

I put my hand up to shade my eyes. I definitely want to see this guy better. "Marcie Henhawk," I say.

"Well, Marcie. You'll have to come and visit us sometime. Isn't that right, Silvia?"

Silvy looks away as if she's focusing on the boat. "Yes, yes of course."

All of a sudden Silvy sounds like some kind of maid or something. She's definitely talking in this English accent. I figure he's got her going to debutante school or something.

"Do you think your little friend would like to come with us to the motor home? Maybe she would like to have a few drinks." He turns and looks at me. "Have you ever had a mai-tai before?"

"Oh, of course," I say. This just blurted out.

"No," Silvy says. "She can't. She's got to dance in the powwow, don't you Marcie?"

"Well. . ."

"*Don't you Marcie!*"

"Yeah," I say. "Maybe we can have some My-Lai's later. After I finish dancing."

They're behind me when we walk back toward the arbor. The crowd noise and my jingles drown out some of the things they say. I hear Silvy utter two or three "don't's" but when we separate she goes with him. I watch them walking up a steep hill into the woods. Silvy must need help because he pushes her up the hill with his hands on her bottom.

Boom, boom, boom, boom, boom, boom-boom.

I stand in the crowd and watch a blur of fluorescent red, blue, pink and chartreuse feathers. It's the men's fancy dancers. They step high, twirl and fall into leg splits to the beat of the drum.

"How about those fancy dancers," the announcer says. "Let's put our hands together and let them know we appreciate them. All nations Inter-tribal next. The Creator likes it when we're dancing so let's keep Him happy. Everybody dance."

I pick up on the singing. I wait until I feel the spirit of the drum. I ease out into the circle. No sense attracting all kinds of attention. I'm supposed to lose points for not being in the Grand Entry. Maybe I'll get lucky and they didn't notice. There's zillions of dancers here. I'll bet I wasn't even missed.

I've got my jingles swaying in a nice rhythm when Darrin Beans comes up. This is the first time I've seen him since school let out. But I know he's had his eye on me. I pretend not to notice him. No sense appearing anxious. Especially with Delbert around.

"Sek:on, Marcie."

I'm trying to move like a cloud. "Se:kon, Darrin." I keep my step clean and sure.

"Kia'tara:se."

Suddenly I'm glad I know the language. He says I have a nice appearance. "Katoria:nerons," I say: I am moved.

"Kattats," he says: I present myself.

He increases his step and draws away from me. He looks so handsome in his traditional outfit. He's got grouse feathers swaying on top of his head like daisy petals. A hawk, circle-bustle pulses in unison with his elegant, manly stride. Traditional dancers tell a story when they dance. I wonder what kind of story he's telling me. He turns and sways toward me then swooshes away like an eagle in flight. He pretends not to notice me but I know he did this to get my attention. Maybe he's telling me a bed time story. I giggle to myself.

Suddenly, Delbert runs up. "I got some real bad news for you," he says standing directly in front of me.

"Get out of my face," I say, craning to look at Darrin.

"Silvy's dead!"

Boom, boom, boom, boom, boom, boom-boom.

I just stand there, unable to move. I feel Delbert's arms around my shoulders. Good thing he does that because my legs are all rubbery. "Don't crush my jingles," is all that comes out. Everybody must know about Silvy because they stop the dancing.

Delbert takes me over to Mum. She's really puffing away on a cigarette. She lets me sit in the folding chair and hugs me. I smell stale tobacco. I feel water from her tears dripping on my neck. I try to talk to her but my throat's got this big lump in it.

"We thought you drowned too," she whispers. "Somebody said they saw you with Silvy and her stepfather-Dad down at the spot where she drowned."

"I *was* with them," I croak. "They wanted me to come to their motor home and have some My-Lai's with them. I went to dance instead."

"Silvy's stepfather-Dad was really upset. They found him asleep. They said that when they took her body to him, he threw up and almost fainted."

Powwow committee members took a long time to decide about the powwow. They even left their trailer office and went into the woods for spiritual guidance. Their leader finally came out and told the loudspeaker guy what was going to happen. They de-cided to honour Silvy by dedicating the whole powwow to her.

They said she came from off the reserve and wouldn't want this festive occasion to stop.

"Ladies and gentlemen," the loudspeakers crack. "The powwow will commence after an honouring dance for Silvia Longfish."

Silvy got honoured by almost everybody. Before her dance ended there were even white people going around the circle. I guess when you drown it's a big thing. Even when you know how to swim.

I go over to the river. I stand where Silvy stood. A tear rolls off my cheek. I pray to the water spirit not to be too harsh with her. She was my best friend. I pull off my centre jingle. I drop it into the water. I hear the drum start up.

Sharlene Wilson Photo

About The Author

RICHARD G. GREEN was born at Lady Willingdon hospital in Ohsweken, Grand River Territory in 1940. He went to school and grew up in Ontario and New York state. While in California, he began studying writing in the late 60's and in 1973 began contributing short stories to *Indian Voice*, an urban Indian monthly magazine published at the San Jose Indian Center. His stories articles and cartoons have appeared in Native publications and literature anthologies in Canada and United States. In 1987, he became a regular contributor to the "Our Town" column in the *Brantford Expositor.* This is his first published collection of short stories. He lives on the Six Nations Reserve where he creates writings for the North American Indian media.